In the
RIGHT PLACE
A Christmas Novel

Douglas Knick

Ten|16
PRESS
www.ten16press.com - Waukesha, WI

Dedicated to Ella, my granddaughter. By the grace of God and the love of Christ, may you always be in the right place.

You are in the right place if you are poor in spirit,
You are in the right place if you mourn,
You are in the right place if you are meek,
You are in the right place if you are hungry and thirst for justice,
You are in the right place if you are merciful,
You are in the right place if you are pure of heart,
You are in the right place if you are a peacemaker,
You are in the right place if you suffer persecution for justice sake.

Greg Boyle, SJ, suggested that a more exact translation of the Beatitudes would be, "You're in the right place."

(www.creighton.edu/CollaborativeMinistry/findinggod-text.html)

CHAPTER 1

GERMANTOWN, MN 1962 POPULATION: 892

"I don't care what he said; we should put it out right away." The force of her words drove everyone against the back of their chairs and threatened to shake the dust free from the light fixtures that hung above the table.

"Don't talk so loud, he's in the next room."

"Really, do you want him to hear you?"

With the greatest of ease, the conversation, despite her presence, shifted from the first person to the third person.

"She doesn't care."

"Well, she should."

"Why should she care, she is not officially a member of the board. Besides, what choice does he have, she's the church secretary. He knows he can't fire her; no one will ever take that position."

"What you meant to say was, 'What choice do *we* have?'" The truth set in with each man in the room as the conversation shifted back to the man on the other side of the door.

"I don't understand why you are all afraid to voice your opinion on this matter, I've heard you disagree with him on other matters." Again, her words were forceful and cutting.

"Maybe we all agree with him. Did you ever consider that?"

"I can't believe that. There is no way you all support the idea of waiting to display…" Rozella Pagel fell silent the moment the copper doorknob screeched as it rolled to the right. The group of ten council members and Rozella were seated on wooden straight back chairs along both sides of the far end of a large handmade oak table. Many joked that the table arrived on the first boat that sailed from the old country.

It wasn't that Rozella was by nature aggressive. Her disposition was the result of nurture or, at the bare minimum, unfortunate experiences that were no fault of hers. If given the option she would prefer, like every other woman in town, to be dependent upon a man to care for her financially and emotionally. She would prefer to busy herself with knitting or sewing a new dress for the next social outing. The truth was, Rozella's 1907 treadle-operated Singer sewing machine rocked the plaster from the dining room wall weekly as she mended her thread barren clothes.

As much as women complained about their husbands, she wished she had a husband to complain about. Buck, as family and friends called him, had been mauled to death by a bull as Rozella looked on in horror twenty-six years ago. The story goes that Buck entered the cow pasture three sheets to the wind early one spring morning. At that time of year, the frost was working its way out of the ground each day only to freeze again each night. The most treacherous spots were in the shallows alongside the barn where the sun had not yet made an appearance. Rozella tried to stop

Buck, but once he set his mind to something, even when intoxicated, he could not be stopped. Initially, the bull ignored Buck, which made Buck throw all caution to the wind and act more aggressive. Even though he was drunker than a skunk, Buck, with the skill of a gymnast, maintained his balance on one leg while he elevated the other leg to shoulder height and placed his foot in direct contact with the bull's backside. Before Buck's leg returned to the ground the bull spun around and had his head, complete with two nasty horns, inches from Buck's groin area.

According to Rozella, Buck went into the pasture to move the bull to an enclosed paddock. Buck roused himself from the lumpy bed at sunrise, with less than two hours of sleep, shouting that it was time to turn out the heifers and it was too early in the year for them to encounter the bull.

The accident, if it could be labeled as such, occurred in the blink of an eye but finished in slow motion. The bull placed his head and nose strategically between Buck's legs, lifted him off the ground and drove his backside into the planks of the barn. With the wind knocked out of his body he dropped like a ragdoll over the bull's head. The bull's horns effortlessly pierced his ribcage with the same ease as a pitchfork slicing through hay. A simple swing of the beast's head hurled Buck's semi-conscious body twenty feet away from the barn. Rozella watched in horror as the bull made sport of her husband's body, tossing the carcass into the air and trampling the 250 pounds of mass into the frozen manure as though it was a worm. The bull moved with the form and grace of an athlete. As she watched, Rozella couldn't help but think of Max Schmeling. Buck would cozy up next to the radio and listen as Schmeling,

Heavyweight Boxing Champion of the World, would pummel his opponents. Mesmerized by what her eyes couldn't hide with a blink it occurred to Rozella that the bull labored to even the score, to extract a pound of flesh for every time a drunken Buck struck or lashed out against any of the cows in the herd. Buck's body was unrecognizable - no longer in the form of a human, completely empty of life and quickly being drained of any blood. The bull lumbered to the far edge of the barn where he watched as Rozella cautiously opened the gate and entered the pasture. With no displays of aggression, no cues of threatening to attack, Rozella took her place next to the mangled corpse that was once her husband and used the voice that only minutes earlier evaporated to summon Junior and instruct him to run and fetch the neighbor.

The year that Rozella's life began to unravel was 1936 and she was but thirty-two years young. Before the morning sun had a chance to tackle the thin layer of frost she found herself alone on a farm with four kids, the oldest, Junior, thirteen and the youngest, Viola, two. Despite family and friends trying to help keep the farm alive, operating 160 acres of rental property without Buck was unrealistic. The only option was to abandon the two-story farmhouse for a two-bedroom apartment above Germantown Zeitung, a weekly newspaper covering local and national news. Ironically, it was the Zeitung that would announce Junior's death during the final days of WWII, and it was the same newspaper, renamed the Gazette to calm fears of German alliance following WWII, that would announce the death of Rozella's third born child, and last male offspring, Herman, during the opening days of the Korean Conflict.

The church, in the summer of 1936, found itself in need of a secretary. Partly out of charity and partly because Rozella demonstrated the ability to maintain confidentiality, she was hired. Now, some twenty-six years later, Rozella had become an institution within the institution of the Lutheran Church, specifically, First Lutheran Church.

She had seen Pastors come and go. Some stayed too long and others left prematurely. Similar to the other males in her life, some of these pastors fell short of her expectations; they were a disappointment, while others abandoned her, or so it felt. For these reasons, she was comfortable telling Pastor Fischer what she thought.

He carefully turned the copper knob and pushed the door inward; the screeching noise, like a schoolteacher slapping a wooden ruler on the desktop, demanded silence. Pastor Fischer smiled as he closed the door behind him, fully aware that his presence, like a tornado on the prairie in the sultry heat of summer, sucked up the voices of everyone in the room. Before he took his seat at the end of the table he apologized for the interruption. Even though it wasn't an emergency, he used the late-night visitor to the church office as an opportunity to allow the council members time to discuss the issue at hand. He knew that some of the members would speak more freely if he was not present. It wasn't a matter of intimidation, but respect. In the mind of some, to disagree with the pastor was a sign of disrespect.

"No need to apologize Pastor, we know you are very busy, and we know that the needs of the congregation can be great."

Even before Walter Stark provided justification for the pastor's absence, Pastor Fischer knew that Walter would be the first to speak and his words would be positive in nature if not affirming. Walter attempted to put a positive spin on everything. Unfortunately, that was Walter's method for avoiding truth or, what some might call, reality. This methodology had forced Walter to file bankruptcy on his farm and it was still to be determined if his marriage would survive.

Reality or truth, the past month and a half was not only an issue for Walter, everyone struggled to find clarity. A fog of uncertainty blanketed the entire country. The Cuban Missile Crisis challenged national and local security and called into question the future. Events seventeen hundred miles away altered the behavior and decision-making process of many people and even though the Cuban Missile Crisis threat and fear of a global holocaust had passed, those thirteen days continued to impact people, both consciously and unconsciously.

In the days and weeks following the Cuban Missile Crisis, First Lutheran Church was experiencing a similar overflow of parishioners attending worship. Church members whom Pastor Fischer had only seen in attendance on Christmas or Easter morning squished into the pews. Other members who attended all the social functions of the church but never Sunday morning worship filed in and found a place beneath the balcony. Individuals who Pastor Fischer knew well from the coffee shop and community events but were identified as guests and visitors to Sunday morning worship snuck in as the opening hymn was sung. The offering plates had never been so full. It was such an exciting time for the church, despite the threat of the unknown, that the previous month the church council discussed the idea of forming an evangelism committee in order to reach out to all the new people attending church.

The events of late October not only drastically altered the church council's opinion concerning welcoming new members, but it also shifted their opinion related to the pastor's behavior.

The sturdiness of the church pews had not been tested in such a manner since Johann Stratmann's funeral, which occurred less than a month prior to Pastor Fischer's arrival; two years ago next week. Johann, Doc as he was known by young and old alike, had been retired, officially for twenty-two years, but unofficially he never retired. On his seventy-fifth birthday the town gathered at the ballroom to thank Johann for his service to the community. He was the doctor who cured the sick, cared for the elderly, sat with the dying, and delivered ninety-nine percent of the children born in the last fifty years in Germantown. He was one of the few individuals in town that both Lutherans and Catholics alike agreed never made religion an issue when treating patients. Therefore, when Doc took his final breath just days before Halloween and was buried on All Saints Day, every pew in First Lutheran Church was stressed beneath the weight of Germans who loved their food. Lutherans and Catholics alike pressed tightly against one another, something only witnessed on the dance floor at the ballroom, in order to pay their respects to old Doc. The day of the funeral, businesses closed their doors early and school was dismissed at noon so that everyone could attend. When the service started, a bit of tension hung in the air. It was All Saints Day and some feared that Pastor Pitzler might seize the opportunity and use the pulpit to recall Luther's nailing of the 95 Thesis' to the Wittenberg Church doors. Pastor Pitzle surprised everyone and used the pulpit to preach how God used the gifts and talents of Johann Stratmann to bridge the gap that can separate Christians.

During the last week of August, Pastor Fischer ordered a baby Jesus for the nativity scene the church proudly displayed each Christmas in the front yard of the church. The council was furious that the pastor spent fifteen hundred dollars without their approval. Members of the council were not placated by the excuse that the sale price was only good for a twenty-four-hour period. Pastor Fischer was adamant that the fifty-inch, ceramic, marble base baby Jesus would serve as a welcoming piece. It would certainly set First Lutheran Church apart from the local Catholic Church and their plastic baby Jesus figurine.

The uptick in people attending and interested in the church the past month and a half made the pastor's purchase seem ingenious. The timing for Pastor Fischer couldn't have been better; muffled voices were questioning his youthfulness, his methods, and his preaching. Church council meetings were lasting late into the night as every clerical action was scrutinized. The voices of critique were silenced for the moment and others could be heard whispering, "Would people rather belong to the plastic church or the ceramic church?" Pastor Fischer however, felt no need to justify the purchase. He explained his behavior by saying, "The Christ child should be presented in the best manner possible."

The church council members slowly came to terms with the purchase of the ceramic baby Jesus but were unable to reach a decision when to place the baby in the Nativity, so they scheduled a meeting for later in week of Thanksgiving. The Nativity display, complete with characters and animals, was scheduled for construction the Saturday after Thanksgiving. Pastor Fischer supported that plan but was adamant that the baby Jesus should not make an appearance until Christmas Eve.

The muffled voices began again, "Fifteen-hundred dollars for two church services?"

CHAPTER 2

Pastor Fischer pulled a cloth from the rag bin. It was a former dishtowel stained yellow from years of use and it was embroidered with a hen and chicks. Using a thick layer of furniture polish, Pastor Fischer glided the towel across the slick surface and, as he did, it appeared the chicks were chasing the hen across the table. He used evenly measured, consecutive circles and made sure that no dust or dirt particles remained. And even though no actual blood was spilled, no amount of elbow grease could remove the bloodbath that occurred across, over, and around this handmade table.

Every pastor, at some point in his ministry, experienced and then marveled at how Christian folks could behave in such unchristian ways. It never ceased to amaze young pastors, even though they were forewarned, how once the church council doors were shut that all decorum, all respect, and all civil behavior was set aside. In his short five-year tenure as an ordained clergy person, Pastor Fischer had been on the receiving end of overly harsh words. What frustrated him was that in both cases the "feud" had nothing to do with the Gospel and the sanctity of God, but everything to do with human tradition.

Viewing his reflection in the tabletop he concluded that last night had been no different. His angst from the previous evening centered on the hypocrisy of the church elders who, rather than setting a good example, became like everyone else attempting to rush the arrival of Christmas. Advent was a time of preparation, but people don't like the wilderness journey from Thanksgiving to Christmas Eve. He felt it was his calling to remind the people, the elders of the church, that God arrives on his own time and he can't be rushed. It was his calling to prepare them for the blessed event, the arrival of the baby Jesus.

He was polishing the table in preparation for the arrival of area Lutheran pastors, who gathered Tuesday mornings to discuss the text for Sunday. Occasionally they also shared the ups and downs of the previous week and a few words of encouragement. Although he could really use some right now, rarely did the meetings include giving advice. The young pastors lacked the experience to be able to provide much wisdom and the older pastors understood the value of silence.

Pastor Fischer gave the table one last spot check and sighed, "Shit." Immediately he regretted his accidental slip of the tongue. Such words became a part of his vocabulary when he was frustrated, literally at his wit's end.

Behind him a throat cleared. Startled, the pastor felt sweat begin to race to the pore ducts of his armpits. Surely whoever was behind him heard him swear . . .

Slowly turning around, he breathed a sigh of relief before he even saw who it was. The voice was recognizable and belonged to someone he trusted.

"I decided to drive over a bit early to unload, but based

on that manure dribbling from your mouth I guess you need to go first."

As he spoke he waved his hand in an effort to convince Peder to accept the very words he himself didn't believe, "It's nothing, just a late night."

"Hey, I know you better than that, it is something or you wouldn't be polishing the table."

Pastor Fischer couldn'thide asmile. "Yeah, you're right, it is something."

"Well, you going to share it or take up a new profession of staring in Pledge TV commercials?"

"The honeymoon is over."

"You and Katie have problems?"

"No, nothing like that, it's here at First Lutheran. Remember how Professor Forde described the initial period of serving a church as a honeymoon? Everyone is polite, respectful and even open to the pastor's ideas. Well, that all came crumbling down last night."

"What happened?"

"Long story short. I purchased a new baby Jesus figurine for the Nativity scene. Due to the high price of the figurine the council wants to place the baby in the manger immediately."

"But, it's Advent not Christmas," Pastor Olsen said.

"Precisely! But that's not the feeling among the majority of the council."

"The honeymoon ended for me the day I asked if I could paint the green walls in the living room of the parsonage blue."

Pastor Peder Olsen served Peace Lutheran Church the next town over. Peder Olsen and Emil Fischer had been classmates in seminary and relished the idea to do ministry in neighboring congregations. Peder was five years into his first call and while the two churches were less than seven miles apart they had a totally different composition.

Peace Lutheran Church, the Norwegian Lutheran Church, located in Fertile Grove, a town on the edge of the river valley, was comparable in size to First Lutheran Church. Although the entire region was composed of immigrants from northern Europe there was a significant difference between Swedes, Norwegians, Germans, and the Finns who pushed much further north, when it came to the practice of religion. Theology was one thing, putting that theology into practice was something else entirely. Peder and Emil had discussed on various occasions that it was not only ethnicity that separated these groups, which it did, but also the sanctity of practice that affected how the people viewed themselves and others.

Two and a half years into his first call the district office contacted Emil and asked him to consider interviewing at First Lutheran Church. The Bishop, nine times out of ten, discouraged newly ordained pastors from leaving their first call before the end of three years, however, he recognized the gifts Pastor Fischer possessed and what First Lutheran Church needed. The church had been labeled a "tough" congregation as the members tended to wear out pastors who, subsequently, left broken and questioning their calling. The Bishop determined that the church needed a seasoned pastor who could weather the storm, but the church council refused to pay the salary necessary to attract such an individual. Consequently, the district office concluded that Pastor Fischer, who was theologically sound and savvy when working with challenging situations, might be the perfect fit. Aware of the history of this particular congregation, Emil agreed to interview anyway. He decided that if the congregation did not extend him the call the interview was always good practice.

As he lumbered up from the river valley in his 1951 Studebaker, twisting and weaving first to the right and then left as the road gracefully wrapped around all the farm sites, Pastor Fischer decided that First Lutheran Church and the community of Germantown might be a good fit. He understood these folks. Although he spent his childhood years a hundred miles from Germantown he had been raised in another German ghetto. The comments offered, and the questions posed by the call committee could easily have originated from his parents or grandparents. By the time he reached the ridge and the rich fertile soil that produced bumper crops year after year, he prayed that if the people of First Lutheran offered him the job that God would bless him with the gifts and patience needed to minister to the people.

Now two years later the word, "shit" still fresh in his mouth made him wonder if it was too much like home and for that reason the people were rejecting him and his efforts. As Jesus said when he returned to Nazareth, "Truly I tell you, no prophet is accepted in the prophet's hometown."

Peder's efforts of discernment were interrupted as the other pastors drifted into the library for the meeting and took their place at the table. The task before them was larger than most Tuesday mornings; in addition to the texts for Sunday there were the Thanksgiving texts to analyze. On the surface it would appear that Thanksgiving and worship was a natural fit, making the sermon for Thanksgiving something that should practically write itself. Reality offered quite a different picture. The assigned texts were the same every year and the Gospel lesson about ten lepers didn't compliment the shallow Hallmark gospel of 'just be happy and thankful.' Unfortunately, with the busyness of two sermons to write, hospital calls to complete, and shut-ins who expected a visit, time was not available for Pastor Fischer or any pastor to discuss weekly struggles.

With both hands busy performing the duties of pastoral care and ministry and no time available for reflection, for discernment, for prayer, the word, "shit" remained fresh and close and infuriating.

CHAPTER 3

The copper fixtures on the chandeliers hanging high above the empty pewter chalice on the altar vibrated beneath the weight of the final cluster of cords the organ bellowed. Slowly the echoing sound died as bodies in the pews absorbed the particles of vibration. In the momentary silence at the end of the Thanksgiving service, Pastor Fischer took his place at the foot of the chancel and reminded the congregation that pie and coffee awaited them in Luther Hall. He tucked the hymnal between his bicep and chest, folded his hands and invited the people to share the table grace before descending to the basement. "Come, Lord Jesus, be our guest, let this food to us be blessed."

He never understood why some folks completed the table prayer with the words, "let these gifts to us be blessed" when it only made sense to be giving thanks for the actual food about to be consumed. "...let this food to us be blessed" was the appropriate wording. He was pleased to discover that the people of Germantown, both Lutheran and Catholics, along with a small handful of Baptists, recited the prayer the proper way.

Saucer plates held healthy slices of pumpkin or apple pie adorned with tablespoon sized dollops of whipped cream. The cream, skimmed from the top of milk cans and whipped into a smooth, creamy, rich substance, originated from the Damhof Dairy operation five miles north of town. The sunburned orange color of pumpkin outnumbered the apple three to one. Kids racing to the front of the line grabbed a plate and a glass of grape Kool-Aid and darted off to a side room where they could converse in private about kid's stuff. The adults carefully balanced their plates and cups of dark, rich egg coffee as they made their way to the tables.

While most of the people forgot the pastor's message about giving thanks, the noise level was 9.8 on the Richter scale as conversation filled the space. At some of the tables people bellowed with laughter while at other tables a single voice whispered some juicy details of a love affair blooming, a marriage withering, or a child suspended from school. Of course, there was always that one table shrouded in silence. That table tended to attract those who didn't fit into any group, those who were first time visitors, and those who thought they selected the seat of their own free will but failed to acknowledge that they were actually directed to the table by those who refused to acknowledge their presence.

Even though more than nineteen hundred years separated them, Luther Hall was not that far removed from the village Jesus entered as he passed along the border between Samaria and Galilee. People spent so much time busying themselves with life that most did not notice Jesus. Similarly, few noticed that missing from the basement was the pastor and the council members.

It had been suggested at the special meeting on Monday evening, although no one could remember by whom, to cast a secret ballot concerning the timing of placing the baby Jesus in the manger. But, before anyone could respond, and before Rozella could fetch scraps of paper and pencils, the council president, Jerome Lietzau, buried the idea. Jerome, with his thick gruff German dialect howled, "We have never done a secret ballot and we ain't gonna start now. There are no secrets in this church. Besides, it's good to know, to see, who your allies are."

The pastor stirred for a moment considering a response. The word allies, fresh on the heels of the events in Cuba, invoked images of war. He wondered, did the council members identify this as a battle? If there were allies did that mean some members were the enemy? Jerome's words made Pastor Fischer very nervous. He was not naïve, he understood the politics at work, but it still made his skin tingle.

As the meeting ended Monday evening both sides knew they needed to focus their energy on convincing Walter to raise his hand with them, but the more interesting dynamic, at least as Pastor Fischer viewed it, was Karl and Liam Mueller.

Karl and Liam Mueller were brothers separated by twenty-nine years and ten other siblings. Karl was the whoops on the front end of creating a family. Mamma Mueller just turned sixteen when the stirring in her belly made it impossible to keep any food down and dad was eighteen, closing in on nineteen. Liam was the whoops on the back end of the family unit. At the age of forty-five mamma knew another baby was on the way before there was stirring and dad, forty-eight, continued to ask the ridiculous question, "How did that happen?" The closest sibling in age was eight and in second grade when the bassinet was carried into the house and the kids living at home cried, "Seriously, another one?"

When Liam was born, Karl and his wife had already been married for eleven years and had children older than Liam. Those kids, although technically identified as nieces and nephews, in spirit became Liam's "siblings." And in a similar manner Karl served as Liam's father figure since their father, Karl Sr., suffered a stroke the week Liam took his first steps. Within less than six months Liam walked better, further, and faster than his father. Karl Sr., who had enjoyed life and especially his children and grandchildren, became an angry and bitter man who prayed to die. When his death wish was not granted, he became more dependent on everyone else to meet his most basic needs. By the time Liam no longer needed diapers or someone to wipe his bottom, Karl Sr., an independent, barrel-chested man, once as strong as any professional weight lifter, relied on others to take care of his most basic needs.

Karl, a Jr., but a suffix he refused to connect to his name, became the saving presence for Liam. His home just across the field from the Mueller homestead became a sanctuary, a safe place to retreat when the pressure in the old farmhouse grew too great. In the end, it really was about more than a place to retreat, it was the trust that Karl displayed that assisted Liam during his adolescent years. Similar to every other stoic German family in Germantown the message wasn't necessarily conveyed with words. Frequently, what wasn't said provided the most powerful lessons. The relationship between Karl and Liam defied all the limitations of definitions. Therefore, it was quite a surprise on Monday when Karl registered a vote one-way and Liam another.

At the conclusion of the Thanksgiving Service Pastor Fischer wondered, as he watched the congregation sift like grains of sand in an hourglass towards the basement and the council members towards the library, if Liam's support for not placing the figurine in the manger immediately would be altered after two days of speaking with Karl.

Tiny specks of red phosphorus from the tip of matches sprayed sparks across the table like fireworks on the Fourth of July. Five glass ashtrays were placed down the center of the table, each comfortably within reach of anyone who lit up a cigarette or cigar. Pastor Fischer was the only pipe smoker in the room and, after carefully packing the bowl with "Half and Half Pipe Tobacco," he pulled from his shirt pocket a "Diamond wooden match."

Through the blue filtered cloud of nicotine, the council members cautiously looked first at those directly across the table and then quickly, to avoid detection, scanned Walter's face to determine if they could guess how he would cast his vote.

Walter was too busy sprinkling "American Spirit" tobacco onto a paper wrapper to notice he was the focus of everyone's attention. As his tongue wet the sticky portion of the wrapper his eyes drifted upward, and he realized that everyone was staring at him. Without thinking his fingers rolled the cigarette and then stuck it in his mouth, and there it rested, in the right corner unlit. He started to speak, "Whaaa..." but stopped and, realizing what he had done, carefully removed the unfiltered cigarette from his mouth and said with a chuckle, "Oh yeah."

Jerome took that as his cue to start the meeting. "Well let's get started, pie awaits. All in favor raise…"

"Aren't we going to hear reasons for and against?"

Jerome didn't wait to discern who spoke he merely responded. "Waste of time. In fact, as I think about it, voting is a waste of time. We only need to ask Walter for his vote. Walter, what ya say?"

Liam, the youngest member of the council spoke softly as though worship was still happening, "What if someone, or maybe even several of us, changed our minds?"

Walter straightened and popped the unlit cigarette back in his mouth as he spoke. "What? Someone changed his vote? Then I don't need…"

"Not so fast, we don't know any such thing." Jerome spoke with both hands raised as though trying to stop a runaway horse from bolting past him.

Liam's voice grew in volume, "That's my point, we don't know and therefore we need to vote."

"Look, kid…" The crease between his eyes deepened as Jerome leaned forward.

Karl spoke for the first time, "Careful there, Litz, you don't want to get carried away." Litz was Jerome's nickname originating from his early adolescent years. Since the name Litz had been tag teamed with tits, it was not a complimentary invocation. As a kid, Jerome was husky, the word his mom associated with his body mass, but it was just a polite way of saying he was fat. His chest was flabby, and it appeared that, similar to females his age, he was developing breasts. As a result of the harassment he endured, until the labors of farm work yielded muscle in place of flab, only those whom Jerome trusted, and maybe feared, were allowed to call him Litz.

At the other end of the table the pastor blew a series of smoke rings and cleared his throat, which was enough of a distraction to focus everyone's attention back to the vote.

Jerome started with what he was confident everyone could accept as truth. "I got a feeling the pie is going fast. You know how some of the guys like a second, even a third, slice." Watching the heads nod he plowed on. "All those in favor of placing the baby Jesus in the manger starting this Sunday raise your hand."

To make sure there was no mistake Jerome counted out loud starting on his left. "One, two, three," he paused for a moment to discern. The problem was Walter's hand. The fingers appeared to be raised, elevated away from the table, signaling a vote of affirmation and yet the base of his palm, his wrist, was still wresting on the tabletop, suggesting something else. "Hey Walter, yes or no? There are no maybes here."

Walter extended his arm halfway across the table and trained his pointer finger on Rozella, although he was speaking to Jerome, "There are other votes still to be counted."

As the pastor listened to Jerome and Walter banter his gaze remained focused on Walter. Walter Stark. He never considered calling Walter anything but Walter. Staring at Walter's profile he remembered a similar scene as he sat with Walter and Sarah in the kitchen of their old farmhouse and watched as tears streamed down his face. The dairy cows, Walter's connections to life, had been loaded on two semi's earlier that afternoon, the hogs were scheduled to be taken the next day, the land would permanently become the property of the bank the following day, and four days out,

Walter would be forced to leave the house his grandpa built, the house in which he entered the world. To make matters worse, Sarah said she had had enough. She questioned if she could continue to live with him. No, he was not a Walt, he was Walter, or, as he had stated previously, his baptismal name was Walther.

Ironically, Walter, whose name means 'the ruler of an army,' never did have to cast a vote because both Liam and H.M. Gerke changed their vote. Liam's vote surprised everyone except Pastor Fischer. No one was surprised by H.M. Gerke's vote - everyone knew his wife would control his vote. She was, after all, Rozella's sister.

With seven votes cast it was determined, baby Jesus would make an appearance Saturday evening at the unveiling of the Nativity. Only apple pie awaited the arrival of council members to Luther Hall.

CHAPTER 4

At nine o'clock Saturday morning an array of people filtered into the church; the cleaning service employees, the volunteer confirmation teachers and the disgruntled confirmation class attendees. In addition to the regular Saturday morning crowd, members of the church council, minus Pastor Fischer, also gathered at the church to construct the Nativity. Their first order of business was coffee. And then they needed to remember where the materials from last year's Nativity had been stored. Eventually, they found the figurines in a back corner at Becker's Repair Garage where they had been stored because it was dry and rodent free and because there was no room at the church.

The neatly stacked pile of lumber that made up the wooden frame practically jumped out and tripped Stanley Dempewolf, which was humorous since Stanley owned the local lumberyard. The problem for Stanley, although he would never acknowledge it, was that, after another evening spent at the bar, his vision at 9:00 a.m. on a Saturday morning was less than twenty/twenty. After last Christmas the materials had been piled on the backside of the garage at the far end of the cemetery, not the first place one would look since it was nearly three-quarters of a mile from the church. The roof for the stable, the length of which was nearly equal to the width of the doublewide garage, remained in one section. The depth of the roof was only two feet, just enough to create the illusion of a stable. While unpacking the pile of lumber that made up the back and sides, several mice' nests and rotten boards were unearthed.

As the crew awaited the arrival of replacement boards from Dempewolf's lumberyard, large snowflakes began to fall. The weatherman, who refused to stake his reputation on the unpredictability of one digit either side of thirty-two degrees, had predicted snow showers mixed with freezing rain. The amount of accumulation would depend on the temperature and when it dipped below thirty-two degrees.

When the men broke for lunch at half past noon, construction of the stable was complete and the freshly fallen snow, heavy with moisture, measured nearly three inches. An inch an hour had fallen and the charcoal colored clouds in the western skies hulking into the valley didn't offer any end in sight.

Heavier and thicker than the snow piling up outside was the conversation inside. The chatter all morning had centered on an accident that had occurred during the middle of the night, which is also why the pastor was not around to help build this morning. The varying accounts were thick with speculation and light on specifics.

So far, the agreed upon details were that Vanessa Hillman climbed out of David's car at 1:30 a.m., thirty minutes after her curfew. After one final kiss, David said he was heading home. His vehicle, a 1950 green Chevy Club Coupe, was spotted some two hundred yards into a plowed field resting on its hood at what was known by the locals as "Lester's curve." According to Katie, Pastor Fischer's wife, who sat with the other wives in the church basement, the pastor received a call at 3:45 a.m. from Sheriff Schuette asking him to go to the Arendt farm place with him to inform David's parents of the accident and that he was being transported to County Central Hospital, in the Twin Cities. After recovering from the shock of waking to pounding on the door at four in the morning and being greeted by the Sheriff and the pastor, David's dad, Steffen, in a fog of emotional instability, decided he would stay home and start milking immediately if Pastor Fischer would transport David's mom to County Central. He would join them as soon as he completed the chores. Since David was an only child, there were no additional arrangements required.

Stories began circulating in the Café early the next morning and were consumed by customers hungry to satisfy their appetite for food and for gossip. They were juicy assertions dripping with tales of debauchery. The rumors covered every unthinkable scenario from drunkenness to sexual escapades. Eventually, these tales overtook the conversation in the basement of the church. One line of chatter was that supposedly David became aggressive, even violent, when he drank. Everyone was fairly certain that there had been a party to celebrate the basketball team's victory over Fertile Grove. Another version was rooted in a baseball analogy suggesting that the young couple had moved well beyond second base. An additional yarn that was gaining wide acceptance in the absence of specifics surrounding the accident was the conjecture that this was not an accident but an attempted suicide. The reason for

Vanessa's tardiness, so the story went, was due to David's feeble attempt to persuade her not to end their relationship.

Katie cleared her throat to attract the ears of the men seated at the first table who took great pride in delivering such gossip as though they, and they alone, possessed the knowledge and therefore the power. She spoke softly, forcing them to be silent. Those seated with their backs to Katie pivoted on their metal folding chairs to look directly at her as she spoke. "The last report I received from Emil, he called shortly after they arrived at County Central, was that David was clinging to life. The doctors stated that if he was not in such excellent physical condition he would not be alive."

The harsh reality of just what was at stake here gripped the throats of everyone and the room fell silent.

Emil always marveled at how skilled Katie was at defusing situations. Her quiet, calm manner was respected and appreciated. Emil was frequently reminded of the writings of Martin Luther who described his beloved Katie in a very similar manner. It was humbling for Emil because he was the pastor and yet, it was Katie who consistently knew what to say and when to say it.

Katie did not share everything her husband told her when he phoned from the hospital. What she didn't describe was how Emil hardly recognized David. His face ballooned from the fragments of glass lodged from the base of his hairline to the dimple in his chin. She never uttered a word that as horrific as David appeared in ICU the real threat was not visible. The cuts, the swelling were surface issues. If he survived, Emil's voice also swelled as he spoke the words, "a huge if," there would be scarred, visible reminders of the accident. But the serious issues were buried deep within his body.

There was internal bleeding, and the blood pooling in his gut originated from multiple locations. There was lung damage, liver damage, and kidney damage. The immediate solution, only a stop gap procedure, a finger in the dike, was the removal of his ruptured spleen. The problem with such an action, Emil explained to Katie, was it compromised David's ability to fight future infections, plus it was an invasion of David's body without addressing the critical points.

Normally strict rules governing visitation lengths in ICU were enforced, but as long as Emil and David's mom stayed off to the side, out of the way, an exception to the rule was permitted. Emil concluded that this unexpected behavior originated with the nurses who were also mothers and did not envision David would survive. If he did awake, if he opened his eyes, the first person he needed to see was not a doctor, but his mother.

The uninterrupted sounds of the machines monitoring David's vitals created a rhythm that made it difficult for Emil to keep his eyes open. The adrenaline high from the events of the morning was giving way to the need for sleep. Not being able to converse with David's mom, as she was consumed with grief, compounded the situation. To replace the enticing desire to close his eyes, Emil resorted to the only thing he could think of, pinching the outside of his leg. Pinching a narrow portion of skin created an irritation that did the trick for all of ten minutes. Before the minute hand on the wall clock, across from David's bed, had measured thirty minutes he was unable to determine if he was actually pinching his leg or if he was dreaming he was pinching his leg. The power of dreaming was an area of psychology only recently gaining the attention of researchers, but Emil knew the power of dreams. When struggling with a sermon he paid attention to his dreams. He was confident, no matter what the research revealed, dreams had the power to reveal ourselves to ourselves.

For a period of time, Emil drifted between varying degrees of slumber. His eyes fluttered open every few minutes for a split second to reveal little more than the gray tile floor and the metal legs of the hospital bed only to be followed by visions of the entire room seen with his eyes shut. Once his eye lids fell heavy and where no longer able to be persuaded to reopen, he entered the world of dreams. But this time his dream revealed nothing about himself, only about David.

Traveling down an unfamiliar, winding, dusty gravel road he should have been apprehensive, but he wasn't. Many of his dreams took place on a road. He always thought that was because he spent so much time in his vehicle making pastoral calls. The radio played "Faded Love" by Patsy Cline. As she whispered the refrain in her honky tonk voice, "As heaven would miss the stars above," David's voice filled the car.

"Pastor, you gotta tell them. You gotta explain the events. You gotta let them know I loved them."

The past tense of love startled him and threatened to wake him completely. As the dream rolled on he entered the next curve of the country road and shook his head slightly to clear his thoughts and remain within the dream and listen.

"Gossipers are already abuzz. Roll down your window and listen to the phone line overhead hum the rhythm of the rumors. The word suicide will become the mainstay and mom and dad will be caught. Pastor, you can't stop the rumors, but you can, you gotta convince my parents that this was an accident."

The clarity of the words delivered by David nearly caused Emil to miss the curve and launch his vehicle into the field. He checked the passenger seat, but it was empty. A check of the rearview mirror did not reflect the body of anyone seated in the backseat. David's voice permeated the interior of the car, yet his body was not present. Dreams defy the logic of reason and so, he went with it.

Emil heard his own voice, "What am I supposed to tell them?"

"The truth. Heat from the vents on the floor of my car pushed a rush of warm air up towards the seats. It ruffled the tassels of Vanessa's scarf and they floated as though dancing to the music on the radio. I reached to retrieve the scarf; I knew it would be saturated with her perfume and return her presence to the car. I only pulled my eyes from the road for a second but that was the second Lester's curve jumped up and took control of the car. I felt the front left tire grab hold of the gravel on the shoulder. I jolted upright and firmly took hold of the steering wheel to correct my mistake, but it was too late. Similar to John Glenn in Friendship 7, I too was orbiting, spinning above the earth. Unfortunately, there was no large body of water to splash down into; I landed in a plowed field upside down causing the car to twirl like a wobbly top two or three more times before coming to a complete rest. While I was penned in the car I replayed the conversation Vanessa and I had only an hour earlier."

"Was she breaking up with you?"

"No." Even without a face to see Emil knew the reply was delivered with a grin.

"Were you breaking up with her?"

"Breaking up? Pastor, I loved her." The grin and light-hearted tone were replaced with a serious tenor. "And I loved the life that was growing within her."

"Sh..." even in the dream, Emil stuttered, "she, she was pregnant?"

"Yes."

Emil's dream world drilled to the core of his brain and drove him to lament, "Oh, David." As the winding gravel road to the dream appeared to never end Psalm 22 filled his inward voice, "My God, my God, why have you forsaken him..."

Framing the conditions of a plea deal with God, David's voice interrupted Emil.

"Isn't there something in the Bible about the sins of the father upon the children?"

"Yes, in Exodus, it says, "The sins of the father shall be cast upon the third and fourth gener..."

"Ya well, I guess that's what happened." David laughed sarcastically before he continued, "Vanessa and I said early on that we were not going to be like our parents. Both of our parents had a shotgun wedding. We were going to be different. We had plans. Graduate from high school, then college, careers, and..." his voice trembled as his sentence ended abruptly.

As he waited for David to continue, Emil's thoughts leaped to the promise God bestowed upon Abraham, "Your descendants shall be as numerous as the stars in Heaven." Even in the midst of sin, God was busy working grace. David, and now his child, would be counted among the stars in Heaven.

The voice continued, "Well, that all ended the moment life began to grow within Vanessa. The reason I was so late dropping her off was because we were making plans for the future. We had decided that both of us, no matter what anyone said, would finish high school. Rather than attend college I would ask dad if I could join him on the farm thinking we could expand the milking herd, raise a few more hogs, and see if we could rent the farm place and the land down the road. Our idea was to get married the weekend after Easter. That way I could finish out the basketball season and Vanessa could continue cheerleading. There was never a question about the future, it would be difficult, but we loved each oth…"

There were no flashing lights yet a siren muted David. An emergency vehicle was approaching but from where? Emil squinted and pressed forward to see through the windshield of the dream car while glancing at the rearview mirror. The wailing decibels continued without any accompanying lights. His knuckles turned white squeezing the steering wheel fearing he was about to crash into something or worse yet, into someone. And then, another sound.

Squish, pause, squish, pause, squish…closer and closer it drew until his right forearm felt a breeze. The feel of the cool air pulled him from his dream world. As his eyes adjusted to the hospital lights, he saw a nurse, with rubber soled shoes, standing beside David's bed fidgeting with the tubing from a machine connected to his arm.

Sensing someone in the room was watching her she turned and said, "The tube was kinked so it set off the alarm. It always sounds worse than it is."

Leaning forward David's mother inquired, "Is there any change?"

"No, he is still in a coma, but that is not necessarily a bad thing. His body needs to remain still so that it might heal."

Glad to be awake and not ready for a repeat visit to dream world, Emil assisted David's mom to the waiting room area for a cup of coffee. Reports were starting to trickle into the hospital that driving conditions in the state were challenging. Snow was moving up from the southwest and the wind was making visibility difficult. David's mom, already a nervous wreck, started to worry about her husband's ability to get into the city. "Thank you for staying here with me, Pastor, I don't think I could handle being here alone."

"I understand. No need to worry, I am not leaving."

"But, there's church tomorrow and if the roads are getting bad how will you get home?"

"I'm not worried. I have done my share of navigating through blizzards. The forecast doesn't sound like this is going to amount to much. Once David's dad arrives and everyone is settled I'll take off for home."

Reaching across the small table she placed her hand atop his and again thanked him. He knew the power of touch and without giving it a thought he placed his other hand on hers and offered a prayer for strength. As he delivered the "Amen" he realized the prayer was as much for him as it was for her.

CHAPTER 5

Prior to leaving the hospital, Pastor Fischer wanted to assure David's parents that David loved them and that he was totally at peace no matter what the future brought, but Emil stopped himself for fear they would inquire how he knew such things. They would never understand the dream, he wasn't sure he understood the dream or that it was rooted in truth. Like marbles scattering in multiple directions on a wood floor, questions rattled forth from his short memory. Was Vanessa with child? Had the two of them actually been planning their future? Did Vanessa leave behind a scarf? Miracles happen, he didn't doubt that, but there is a time and place to share such things. With David still alive, or being kept alive by machines, this was neither the time nor the place to speak of such things. The miracle his parents desired to hear was that of recovery.

Even though it was only mid-afternoon, darkness engulfed his vehicle as Emil left the comfort of traffic, pointed the car to the southwest, and drove straight into the blizzard. It was impossible to determine if it was still snowing or if the snow swirling about was simply wind driven. He considered himself lucky that he was able to align the wheels of the car in the track of a semi ahead of him. Trusting that the trucker would not dip below twenty-five miles an hour, he set his foot against the accelerator pedal to maintain the same speed and froze his leg in that position. To keep his mind alert and not overwhelmed with blizzard fatigue, he crafted David's funeral sermon.

The writing of the sermon had less to do with the dream and everything to do with David's condition. The act of writing a sermon before a person actually died was not something pastors spoke about with congregational members, yet it was a practice widely implemented by clergy members for several reasons. First, there was the matter of time. Generally funerals occur within three or four days after death and, regardless of whether or not there was a funeral, a pastor still needed to prepare the Sunday sermon. Second, and perhaps most important, was the fact that people who attend funerals listen intently to every word spoken.

Even without the knowledge of the conversations that brewed back in Germantown surrounding the accident, Emil was very aware that David's funeral had the potential to exceed the number of attendees that were at Doc Stratmann's funeral. It would be extremely important for him to silence all rumors surrounding the situation and focus on preaching the Gospel.

On the car radio, Patsy Cline crooned her new hit single, "Faded Love." This time it was not a dream. His ear was drawn to every word. "As Heaven would miss the stars above." Was it even conceivable that Heaven might miss a single star? Emil knew exactly the message he was called to preach at David's funeral.

As he pulled into Germantown, Emil wished there was a way for him to thank the trucker ahead of him, but the moment his foot eased off the gas pedal, the back of the trailer disappeared in a flurry of whiteness. Instead, he asked God to guide his angel home safely and he thanked God for delivering him safely to Germantown. But, rather than going directly home, he went to the church. Three miles out of town, or what he thought was three miles, he remembered that the church council members had assembled earlier in the day to construct the Nativity. He couldn't resist the desire to view the Christ child in the manger.

As he approached the corner of 10th Avenue and Church Street excitement rose in his chest. In his haste to arrive, he pushed the pedal toward the floorboard and accidentally caused the rear end of the car to slide to the right. Even in the darkness more than two blocks from the church, the flood lights around the nativity glowed majestically as though something angelic was about to appear.

A cove to the right of the front doors created by an enclosed stairwell provided the perfect location for the Nativity. It was tucked neatly against the brick façade of the building, which helped to offer a break from the northwest winds that followed the hillside. Beyond protecting the Nativity frame and figurines the corner faced the street, so community members did not need to brave the harsh conditions of winter to enjoy the scene. The only question to be answered was, would the Christ child be visible?

Pulling to the curb across the street the pastor smiled as he saw the scene. Each character had been perfectly placed; Joseph and Mary were closest to the manger while the animals were spread out giving the perception that each was making their way to steal a glimpse of the child. The wise men, who did not appear until the twelfth day bearing gifts, were posed the furthest from the manger just inside the parameter of the light's rays. He wondered if Katie had something to do with orchestrating the placement of the figurines. In her quiet manner, she would have been able to convince the workers of the importance of placing each character in the proper position.

He squinted to catch his first glimpse of the Christ child and suddenly he noticed a sharp flash out of the corner of his right eye. Actually, it was more like a light being reflected back into his car by a mirror or maybe a piece of metal. He stared out the front window of the car and was startled when, between waves of snow swirling past the hood of the vehicle, he saw the hood of another car. His first thought was, "My God, I nearly hit another car. What if..." he stopped himself for a second, "if I had not stopped..." He shook his head to clear his thoughts. The questions continued to swirl as though the northwest wind thrust them into his brain. "Was the car there when he pulled up or did it arrive after him? More importantly, was someone inside? Of course someone was, what else would explain the flash. But who, and on a night like this?"

Flipping his collar up he labored to force the top button of his overcoat through the seldom-used slit. He reached his gloved hands for the door handle and, as he leaned his shoulder against the interior of the door, a loud crack greeted the wind and welcomed snow into the car. The door tried to fight back in the wind, tried to keep Emil from entering the world of wintery elements. Rounding the front fender, he carefully stepped between the grill of each vehicle. Less than thirty seconds had elapsed since his face clashed with the first blast of Mother Nature but already his cheeks felt as though they had become a pincushion.

Unable to gain the attention of the person inside the car he rapped on the window. Slowly the window moved downward as the person within cranked the handle around and around. The pastor's first words were apologetic, "I am so sorry, I didn't know another car was here. I am thankful I sto…" He stopped himself as the driver of the car moved closer to the window.

Emil's demeanor changed the moment he saw to whom he was speaking. "What are you doing out on a night like this? And why are you parked here?"

"I didn't know where else to go. I was hoping you would return to the church."

"We need to get you home."

"I need someone I…I can talk to."

"There will be plenty of time for talking, right now…"

"Pastor, did you notice how inviting the baby Jesus looks? I know it is only a doll, but…well, you know…it looks so real. It looks like Jesus is looking right at me."

Emil attempted to take another look at baby Jesus, but the snow was blowing so hard he could barely open his eyes. Unable to get a good visual he ducked his head back inside the car and said again, "We need to get you home. Seriously, the conditions are growing worse."

"But," gripping the steering wheel with both hands, Vanessa fell forward striking the crown of her head on the wheel. After several minutes of silence, or what felt like minutes to Emil who stood against the car, she pushed her body away from the steering wheel and looked directly into her pastor's eyes as she continued her thought, "but can you at least tell me how David is doing?"

Hearing David's name Emil stood up and, forgetting his head was inside the window, he crashed his neck into the door frame. Under normal circumstances, he would not have forgotten where his head was and more importantly, he would have recognized the anguish Vanessa was experiencing, but he was so tired he wasn't thinking clearly. As he stepped away from the car he spoke, "Yes, of course, come inside and we will worry about getting you home later."

A third of the way across Church Street the wind stopped. What moments earlier had been a raging blizzard was nothing more than still, cold air now. Stepping up on what he figured was the sidewalk, Pastor Fischer stopped and took in the Nativity. Vanessa had said it well; it did appear as though the baby Jesus was inviting one to come closer. Even though it was nothing more than a figurine, as they pushed through the snow drifts towards the church door he whispered, "Thank you."

As the key effortlessly slid into the lock he realized that he stood alone. Vanessa had not climbed the three-foot drift that barricaded the entrance; rather she stood staring at the Nativity. Returning to her side he carefully placed his arm around her waist to assist her over the drift but she pushed against him. Without looking at him she asked, "Does God punish people?"

Without answering the question his arm applied pressure to her back with the reassurance that once inside they could discuss the question. But like a mule, her feet didn't move.

"Look at the baby. That is not the face of an angry God." Pivoting into his body she continued to speak without looking up at him. The sweet fragrance of her perfume escaped from inside her Navy Pea coat and it transported him back to the dream when David described Vanessa's scarf on the floor of his vehicle and wanting to smell her again. "Jesus is God, right? Isn't that what you told us in confirmation? I don't understand how that baby could punish humanity for sins committed. Especially when…"

Stepping back, he carefully placed his hands on her shoulders and looked directly at her face in order to convey the seriousness of the words he was about to speak. "I promise you we will discuss these questions indoors, but standing out here in the cold is not doing either of us any good. Plus, I think it would be good if I called my wife to let her know I arrived safely back in town and we should phone your parents to let them know you're safe."

Striding as only a teenager can through the snowdrift she said, "You can call them, but they are going to be mad no matter what you say. They made it perfectly clear I was not to leave the farm."

Safely inside with the furnace working overtime to remove the chill from their bodies, Emil proceeded to describe David's condition as delicately as possible while not avoiding the truth. He held a cup of instant coffee, mainly as a method of warming his hands and not because he enjoyed the taste of what he considered artificial coffee, and he thought about Vanessa's question, "Does God punish people?" Fully aware that this was not a simple yes or no question he worked to understand the context of the question. If the dream from earlier in the day was true he was pretty sure he knew the context for the question already, but he needed Vanessa to say it.

"So why do you think God might punish people?"

"Doesn't the Bible teach that?"

"I don't know, does it?" He could cite several examples, examples that Vanessa would understand: the flood, Sodom and Gomorrah, the account of Jonah, David and Bathsheba. For a second he thought about throwing out the names of David and Bathsheba, but Vanessa did not give him a chance.

"Well, daddy says it does."

"Okay…"

"Daddy said when Spike, my dog, was run over by the milk truck that was God punishing me for not listening to him and mommy."

The hair on the back of the pastor's neck stood straight up like the hair on the back of dog about to defend itself. Even though it was only sixty degrees in the church he felt his skin tingle as beads of sweat surfaced. But again, before he could deliver a single word she continued to speak.

"When old man Pagel was killed by the bull daddy said that was because he was an alcoholic, and he beat his wife, so God beat him and even his sons."

Emil didn't understand how an event of nearly thirty years ago still had a life in the community.

"People always get what they have com'in. Sometimes it just takes God a while to respond, but he always responds."

Setting the empty coffee cup on the desktop he asked, "Do you think David's accident was God punishing him?" He watched her closely as she pushed back in the chair. Her hands rested on her stomach and slowly her fingers rubbed the fabric of her sweater.

"I'm not sure."

His thoughts swirled with all the "proper" theological responses he could share. He pondered how he could challenge the wisdom she absorbed from her father, and invite her to consider other options. But then he considered the possibility that he was naïve, or worse yet, arrogant to assume she could change her position. The words that spewed forth surprised even him.

"When are you due?"

She stared at him. He couldn't read her expression or lack thereof. Finally, she spoke, "Due? I don't understand."

He understood completely that his interpretation of her hand gestures and his question were totally based on a dream, he now realized, he had accepted the dream as gospel. The next few minutes would either prove or disprove the dream and David's voice. If Vanessa wasn't pregnant that would mean…again, he silenced his thoughts. When he eventually spoke, he stared directly at her hands covering her stomach.

"You know, when are you due?" He added a nod to emphasize the point.

The pregnant pause that followed grew and expanded filling the room with tension. The one thing Emil recalled from the pastoral counseling course he took at the seminary was to wait, be patient. Don't speak first after asking a difficult or challenging question. So, with eyes locked on one another as though in a stare down to determine which one would blink first, they sat as though they too, like David, were comatose.

Her gaze dropped first, and she asked, "How did you know?"

Without forethought, he started to say, "David to…" He stopped himself. He could not tell her David told him in a dream. Instead he said, "It's a gift. I can just tell when a woman is pregnant."

She remained unable to look at him as he continued to speak.

"So, you think that God punished David because you and he are going to have a baby? Vanessa…"

She looked up and her head was shaking. "David and I…" She stopped. Her hands were wringing. She started to bob back and forth in the chair. She started again, "It's not…" Again, she stopped. Finally, she completed a sentence. "You don't understand."

"What don't I understand Vanessa? Tell me what I am missing."

"God punishes me by taking away from me those that love me. He punishes the innocent to increase my suffering." Vanessa's cheeks were washed with her tears.

"But Vanessa, David is not any less guilty or innocent than you."

"You're wrong." She continued to bob back and forth, rocking herself.

Emil was totally confused. The only thing he could conclude was that she blamed herself for getting pregnant and that somehow, she believed she was responsible for them having sex. He just couldn't accept that scenario. Vanessa might blame herself for being pregnant, but David was a typical teenager who was equally interested in sex. Finally he asked, "Tell me how I'm wrong?"

"You said *David* and I are going to have a baby."

"Yes, and you confirmed you're pregnant."

"That's true, I am."

"So, how can I be wrong?" He leaned back in the chair and tried to make sense of what she said and what she was trying to get him to understand. He started to shake his head in bewilderment when it finally hit him. "David is not the father."

She never raised her head. Her lack of a response was affirmation enough.

"But if David is not the father, then why were you planning to get married and who is the father?"

Her head jerked back, her eyes widened, "How do you know we're planning to get married?"

He was caught. He already informed her that David was in a coma and never spoke. He also realized that he misunderstood David as he spoke of the father's sins, he assumed…it didn't matter what he assumed, he needed to determine how best to answer Vanessa.

She impatiently pressed him for a reply. "Do you have a gift for this too?"

"Have you ever had a dream only to have it later come true?"

"No, but I have read about such things."

"Well," slowly, carefully selecting each word Emil proceeded, "this afternoon when I was at the hospital I had a dream and in the dream, David came and spoke with me. He wanted me to tell his parents that this was an accident, not suicide. And he spoke of your situation. But I assumed he was the father."

The idea of learning the truth in a dream didn't seem to unnerve Vanessa. She spoke of David's compassion. "When I told him I was pregnant, I fully expected him to dump me, but after he learned the truth he asked me to marry him. He said no one needed to know and that the child would become his child. I refused, I pushed back but he refused to accept any answer but yes. You want to know the really sad thing in all of this, we have never had sex."

"So, who is the father?"

"I...I..." She stuttered and to avoid eye contact she stared at the crack in the corner (of the desk? The floor?) that appeared last winter. "I...I...can't tell you."

"Vanessa, it's okay." Her eyes were now dry but her shoulders shook and it was apparent she was crying within.

She cleared her throat twice before she attempted to speak. The first few words were faint and difficult to hear but as she continued her body straightened and the volume intensified. "He had power over me once, I will not keep giving him power over me by speaking his name again and again."

"Are you saying you were forced to have sex? You were," he paused before speaking the word, "raped?"

Totally rigid and distant as though attempting to speak across an expansive gorge her words arrived at his ears in waves. "It's all my fault and now David is..."

CHAPTER 6

His eyes had been shut for nearly five hours, but his mind never stopped casting images and therefore, the moment the alarm clanged and he stretched to silence the offensive contraption it felt as though he had not slept a single minute. After following Vanessa to make sure she arrived home safely he arrived home to a dark house. It was already after midnight. As his head sank into the pillow his thoughts replayed the events of the previous day while also trying to rework tomorrow's sermon. Vanessa had said she would be in church with her parents and he was determined to offer a word of hope.

Sitting on the edge of the bed awkwardly struggling to fit his foot into his slipper in the dark, he felt Katie's hand caress his shoulder. "I'm sorry I never heard you come home last night. Did you see the note I left by the phone?"

"Note?" He asked as he leaned back and passionately kissed his wife. He didn't need any light to locate his wife's lips.

She warned him in a flirtatious tone as she half-heartedly pushed him upright, "It's Sunday, Emil, don't start something you can't finish until this evening."

"Yes, yes, I suppose you're right." Of course, she was right, she was always right.

"What did you say about a note?"

Listening as he again struggled to slide his swollen foot into his slipper she spoke to the back of his head. "You didn't see the note I left by the phone?"

"No. I didn't turn on any lights."

"Maybe you should switch a light on now, it might help you complete an elementary task."

"My, aren't we judgmental."

"No, not really. I'm only trying to avoid sharing the news." Katie dropped back onto the comforts of the bed and pulled the covers up over her shoulders as though it might provide protection.

"Go ahead, I'm listening." Even though the room was as dark as a cave he turned his body in her direction.

"David's father called last night from the hospital at about 10:30." The weight of the message pressed her deeper into the bed. Through the mattress, she felt his body tighten and she was sure he guessed what was coming. Rather than prolong the agony she spoke the words she wrote on the paper, "David didn't make it."

"Oh God." In the midst of his sadness and grief it occurred to him that at about the same time that Vanessa was blaming herself for the pregnancy and David's accident, David actually took his final breath. He wondered if David's parents had called Vanessa and her family. He decided that the first order of business, once it was light outside, was to check with the Hillman family. He didn't want Vanessa to learn of David's death seated in the pew.

Emil arrived at church shortly before six. Normally he would have started clearing snow, but alterations to the sermon occupied his attention. He was alone in the church until an hour later when he heard the scraping sound of tin against concrete. He figured it was probably Walter clearing the sidewalk. He had just made his last correction to the sermon when Walter's voice echoed up the stairwell and into the church proper, "Pastor, come quickly. Someone stole…" whatever had been stolen was muted by the slamming of the front door.

"Pastor Fischer, the baby Jesus…"

Rushing from his office the pastor met Walter a third of the way down the stairs. Walter was out of breath from shouting and attempting to climb the stairwell two steps at a time. Walter made it a practice for the past several months to arrive early to church to tidy things up before others arrived. He couldn't afford to contribute to the weekly offering as he once had so he found other ways to pitch in. Walter had told the pastor during the first snowfall, the week prior to Thanksgiving, that shoveling snow wasn't much different than scooping out a calf pen, "It's labor intensive, the stuff sticks to the shovel, your back aches from bending over, it looks good when done, but the final product doesn't last very long."

Walter, still holding the scoop shovel in one hand grabbed ahold of the pastor with the other hand and dragged him down the steps and out the front door without saying a single word.

As they skied down the steps Emil tried to get some answers and to caution his handler. "Walter, slow down. What do you mean, stole? What has been stolen?"

Standing on the portion of sidewalk cleared of snow Walter directed the pastor's attention towards the Nativity. "Look for yourself. It's gone, Pastor. It is just plain gone."

Sure enough, the only thing in the manger was a quarter bale of straw spread out to serve as bedding for the baby Jesus. And of course, footprints, several sets of prints leading to and from the manger.

"Walter, did you walk over to the manger?"

"No, sir. I was carefully shoveling making sure not to throw the snow towards the Nativity. I took a break to look at our work from yesterday and I saw it right away. No baby Jesus."

The two men stood still, staring at the empty manger as though, if they waited long enough, baby Jesus might reappear. But of course, it didn't and the freezing temperature bit at the pastor's exposed skin. His ears tingled and his fingers were growing numb.

"It was there last night, I saw it when I left. When I arrived this morning it was still dark. I parked on the side of the church and I never looked at the Nativity."

Walter was dressed for the outdoors with a winter coat, hat and gloves and made no effort to abandon the sidewalk. "Should we call the police?"

"I'm sure Sheriff Schuette will be in church, I'll catch him before the service to see what he suggests we do."

"Who would steal the baby Jesus? And why? My goodness pastor," the volume of Walter's words grew until he was nearly shouting, "the baby Jesus!"

With his hands cupped over his ears looking to the heavens, Pastor Fischer replied, "Good question, Walter. That is a good question."

Emil wasn't sure he had garnered the attention of the worshippers after the opening announcements. A third of the congregation was in shock trying to digest the news of David's death. Another third of the people seated in the pews was watching the Hillman family to see how Vanessa was holding up. And the final third, composed of church council members, among others, was flabbergasted that someone would actually steal the new Christ child figurine, a fifteen hundred-dollar figurine at that. Pastor Fischer could only pray that the sermon would offer a word of hope in what appeared to be a hopeless situation. Which was precisely what he did, prior to the sermon, when he asked the people to bow their heads in prayer, "Let us pray. May the words of my mouth and the meditations of our hearts be acceptable in your sight O Lord. Amen."

Sheriff Al Schuette was familiar with the library and the long conference table. He was actually able to sit in "his spot," the corner of the table with his back to the bookshelves, while looking directly at the door. Al had served a term on church council prior to the arrival of Pastor Fischer. He had been the Sheriff of the county for nearly a decade. Upon his return from the Korean Conflict, having been awarded a purple heart for being wounded in combat and the Silver Star for demonstrating valor on the battlefield, he joined the local police force. Two months later he was asked to consider joining the county law enforcement team. A year later Al became Sheriff when his boss was killed responding to a domestic call.

Every officer has been warned that a domestic call has the potential to be the most dangerous call to encounter. It is dangerous because an officer never knows what might happen when emotions and tempers are pressed to the limit.

Or when judgments are clouded due to the consumption of alcohol. Plus, the scene is the home territory of the individuals involved in the dispute and the potential for weapons to be present is tremendous. Strangely enough, two people who have been fighting with one another can quickly unite and turn against an officer as though somehow, he is the source of the problem.

The call to dispatch that resulted in the previous Sheriff losing his life was particularly dangerous because he was responding to the house of his lover. It turned out that the husband had learned that his wife and the Sheriff were carrying on when he was at work during the day and at bowling league in the evenings. When the Sheriff arrived, the house was dark except for a dim lamp aglow in the living room. Foolishly, the Sheriff entered the house without waiting for backup that was in route from the other end of the county. With his gun pulled he carefully entered the house. Having previously spent many hours in the house he didn't need light to make his way to the living room. To his horror, he found the woman of the house, his lover, tied to a wooden chair and gagged. Without forethought, he rushed to her side to free her without taking stock of the surroundings. Her husband stepped from the hallway armed with a double barrel twelve-gauge shotgun. The Sheriff was unable to retrieve his pistol from the floor before...

The story goes that the husband, intoxicated, wanted to see his competition and so he demanded that the Sheriff strip down to his birthday suit. After laughing at the size of the Sheriff he became enraged that his wife's attraction to her lover had nothing to do with physical curiosity or pleasure. Supposedly, so the bowling alley gang reported for weeks after, with one barrel the husband dismembered the Sheriff and with the other barrel, a few minutes later, he shot him in the chest, all the while forcing his wife to watch.

Al, the young new deputy, arrived on the scene as the second shot rang out. The house still smelled of gunpowder as he stormed the living room. When the ambulance arrived, the husband was handcuffed to the chair that previously held his wife and a sheet soaked with blood covered the sheriff. The paramedics carefully placed the unresponsive body on the stretcher and raced to the hospital.

Al completed the final year of the deceased Sheriff's term and is now serving his second four-year term as Sheriff.

Pastor Fischer walked into the room and Al nodded his head in acknowledgment. Emil had just left Vanessa and the Hillman family and later in the afternoon he would meet with David's parents and extended family to begin preparations for the funeral. In the short period of Pastor Fischer's tenure, he and Al had become good friends. In fact, Al, who was not married, joked that he was waiting for a woman like Katie to come along and sweep all six feet one inch and two hundred and forty-five-pounds of him off his feet. Truth was, and Emil was aware of this, Al refused to allow any woman to get too close because it would never be fair to her. Al had not slept an entire night since his return from Korea ten years earlier. It also would not be fair, he concluded, to deny a woman the opportunity to give birth but there was no way he could envision having a child in the house twenty-four hours a day. Most of his nightmares included the faces of children. In Korea, the true victims were the children. In the hearts and minds of children there was no North or South Korea there was simply family and friends separated and eventually killed because of a silly line, the 38th parallel. Al often wondered what if it was the 40th or the 36th parallel line? Would that result in peace and justice? Would that have kept families from being severed?

Returning to the library from the imaginary farm fields of Korea, Al wiped the smile of empathy from his face for fear someone would misinterpret his intentions.

The assembly of councilmen and Rozella was not an official meeting. Therefore, Sheriff Schuette did not need to wait for Jerome Lietzau to call the group to order or to be recognized as a guest to speak. The moment Pastor Fischer's backside hit the chair the sheriff launched into a review of the facts.

"I reviewed the site and the following is what will appear in the report." He pulled from his shirt pocket a small flip notepad, thumbed through several pages until he located the page he wanted and read, "Three different sets of footprints merge at the manger. It is impossible to determine if the three sets were created at the same time." Sheriff Schuette pulled back from his flip pad and looked about the room before he continued. "I used the word 'merged' because each set of prints appear to originate from different locations."

Before Sheriff Schuette, having returned his attention to the note pad, could read further, Jerome spoke, "Any idea why that might be?"

Al located Mr. Litezau at the opposite end of the table and directed his response towards him, "My opening comments are factual. I think it is important to always establish what we know as fact before we venture into the realm of speculation, which in my profession is extremely dangerous. I leave that sort of stuff for the theologians and the philosophers." He couldn't help but chuckle as he needled Pastor Fischer without the rest of the council fully grasping what just occurred. Most of the members assumed it was a slam against Lietzau.

Lowering his gaze, the Sheriff continued, "From the manger all three sets of footprints move toward the street." Sensing someone was about to inquire, he quickly added, "Again, I can't determine if they moved together or were even in the presence of one another. I just know each set of footprints moved toward the street. Because the city plow came down the street I don't have any idea where the prints lead after that."

The moment it was apparent Sheriff Schuette was done sharing the facts, Walter spoke, "Who would steal the baby Jesus? And why?"

The Sheriff cleared his throat before he spoke, giving himself a few seconds to determine how best to frame an answer. "Please note this is pure speculation. I don't have any concrete evidence and probably shouldn't respond, but since this is church council and I know you will all keep it quiet . . . " He paused before speaking again, "Money."

In unison, three voices echoed, "Money?"

"Someone could sell it?" Walter asked.

"Honestly, based on the description of the figurine provided by Pastor Fischer there is no way anyone could display the figurine and not know they would be caught immediately. About the only other option is selling it," Al explained. "In Minneapolis it might bring four or five hundred dollars."

A hush fell over the entire body assembled in the library. The thought that a fifteen-hundred-dollar item could be sold for four or five hundred dollars was offensive.

"I told you we should have chained it! Didn't I say we need to chain it to the manger?" Stanley pressed his massive chest forward. "I have experience with items walking away from the lumber yard, unless it is nailed down or securely fastened to a nonmoving object, things have a way of growing feet and walking away."

"Listen to yourself, you don't even make sense. Attach the baby Jesus to a nonmoving item - the manger?" Becker said with a partial smile.

The comment brought a laugh from those seated at the table.

Becker paused briefly and then finished his thought, "Sometimes you just have to trust people."

As everyone collected themselves and focused on the matter at hand it was Liam who spoke. "I think the point is, you don't chain the baby Jesus."

H.M. Gerke attempted to shift the conversation away from 'could have' and 'should have' to the present predicament. "Is there any other reason besides money that might serve as the basis for stealing the baby Jesus?"

Sheriff Schuette slid his chair back a foot in order to see behind Rozella and look directly at H.M. Gerke who sat next to his sister-in-law. "What do you have in mind, Marc?"

Marc turned sideways in the chair so he could make eye contact with the Sheriff. "Envy. Or maybe jealousy? The new baby Jesus made the Catholic Church's Nativity look cheap, even silly." Marc sat upright and tall in the chair, proud of his suggestion.

"Are you suggesting that someone from the Catholic Church took the figurine?" Sheriff Schuette asked.

Marc chose his words carefully as he responded to the sheriff, "You mean stole it?"

The sheriff's eyebrows rose as he considered that possibility, but he never spoke. In fact, no one spoke as they absorbed Marc's suggestion. The tension in the library was thick for several minutes. The relationship between the two churches was less than good, but to suggest a member of their congregation could or would do such a thing was difficult to digest.

Jonas Grack broke the silence, "We have the old baby Jesus. Let's display it and the thief or thieves would see that they didn't win." Generally, regardless of the issue, Jonas' voice was heard in union with others, or not at all, unless giving the financial report.

"Yeah, I never thought about the old one, I was so concerned about the one lost," Lietzau chimed in.

Stanley, removing the cigar from his lips long enough to speak, said, "I don't remember seeing the old baby Jesus, did anyone run across it yesterday?"

Before anyone could elaborate, Pastor Fischer clarified, "No one saw it because it is no longer here. After the new one arrived I sold the old one to help defray the cost. A friend from seminary, now serving a small inner-city church, purchased it."

Jonas moved forward to the front edge of his chair, "How much did we get?"

"One hundred dollars."

"What?" He said as he pressed further forward. "It was worth more than that."

"I had no idea what it was worth, but I knew the church in the city couldn't afford more than that. They actually couldn't afford more than fifty dollars but came up with the hundred."

"So, now we don't have any Jesus for the Nativity. Pastor, I feel I have to be honest here, you have not made wise financial decisions and it is dearly costing the church." Jonas felt empowered to speak with such candor since he had served on the council for forty years as treasurer.

First Lutheran Church's financial ledger, in its ninety-seven-year history, had never left the hands of a Grack. Jonas' grandpa, whose name, Herman Grack, appears number eight on the roster of charter members of the church was elected treasurer in 1865, a position he retained for thirty-seven years because he had also held a respected position at the bank. At the time of his death, Jonas' dad was elected to the post of treasurer because, like his father, he too was good with numbers and he worked at the bank. Jonas was commissioned treasurer at the age of twenty-five when his father died unexpectedly but not because he worked at the bank, he didn't, but because people couldn't envision anyone but a Grack being church treasurer.

Liam's soft voice shifted the discussion slightly, "Maybe Pastor Fischer was right. We should have waited until Christmas Eve to display the baby, Jesus."

"What are you talking about? If someone wanted to steal the figurine they would take it on Christmas Eve as well. The point right now is not when we set out the figurine, but that it has been stolen – so what do we do?" Karl wasn't about to let his little brother place the blame on those who voted to display the figurine sooner rather than later or make him look like a fool. From Karl's perspective if Liam felt guilty that was his problem.

Aware that council meetings could deteriorate quickly into something other than constructive, loving, decision-making opportunities, Sheriff Schuette described the next steps the Sheriff's department would take. "I will put the word out and alert the deputies to keep an eye out for the figurine. I will also contact businesses within a hundred-mile radius that might receive an inquiry about purchasing such an item. Finally, I will be in touch and the best thing you folks can do is listen, listen to the conversation on the street. Generally, people who do something like this are prone to want others to know what they have gotten away with. It is more an act of defiance than an attempt to get rich."

"When I hear you say that, I think of kids, pranksters. Are you suggesting it could have been kids who did this?" As a mother, Rozella prided herself on knowing something about kids. Unfortunately, as she aged she became less tolerant of adolescent behavior.

"It's possible, but honestly, right now, anything is possible based on the information I have. Please hear, I am not suggesting that you do any investigative work and certainly don't start accusing anyone of this crime. All I said was listen."

"So, you are basically telling us to do nothing!" As the person in charge, Lietzau elected himself to speak for everyone on council.

The Sheriff stood and started towards the door. He stopped behind Pastor Fischer and, with both hands resting on the back of the wood chair he spoke, "If that is what you just heard me say, then yes, do nothing."

Passing through the doorway he heard Lietzau's voice again, "As a member of this church you would think he would be a bit more considerate and certainly more concerned."

"Look, folks," Pastor Fischer started to stand but thought better of it and remained seated, "it is only the first Sunday in Advent, we have three more weeks to find the figurine and replace it by Christmas Eve. I agree with the Sheriff we need to listen to the talk on the street, in the stores, in the Café, and certainly, in the school. What we don't want to happen is that we start accusing innocent people."

CHAPTER 7

For the first time in six days the church was silent. Pastor Fischer sat in the office and listened, waiting for some sound to fill the vacuum of silence. The first minute was totally blissful but as the second minute rolled into the third the space became unnerving. The squeak from the chair beneath him as he shifted his weight startled him even though he had heard it a thousand times - and a thousand times he told himself he needed to bring an oil can from home to refresh the metal coil. Immobilizing his body, he directed his attention to the absence of noise and he listened; he even tilted his head as though that might improve his hearing. The absence of sound was eventually filled with the noise of memories from the week, like chaff separated from grain, sifting into his memory. The sounds, the noises, were associated with faces. He didn't just hear a sound in the corridors of his mind he saw the sound. It surprised him initially for he never considered or recognized that certain sounds were linked to certain individuals.

Over the course of the previous week, Emil discovered that if he could just detach himself from the moment and listen, the opportunities for learning were unlimited. The village nestled in the bluffs screamed with a plethora of sounds as word spread that David had succumbed to his injuries and that the baby Jesus had been stolen from First Lutheran Church. The snickers swelled in volume when the price of the figurine became public knowledge. The noise started before Emil even left the church at noon on Sunday.

Bar patrons, pressed against the brick façade of the corner bar, stood under a Hamm's sign wishing the doors weren't locked on Sundays. Instead of a drink, they inhaled nicotine, a sad substitute. Burning the cigarette to a nub to take full advantage of the cent and a half just spent, the cohort of men passed an hour making sport of the church people for their foolishness.

One of the men started off with, "Those goody two shoes pass judgment on us for spending our money on beer when they foolishly spent it on a baby doll. How hypocritical is that?" With each word the cigarette tucked into the corner of his mouth bounced up and down and ashes covered the front of his fur-lined winter coat. Occasionally, a glowing red ash would burrow into the inner lining and a gloved hand would pat the amber slag into submission.

Attempting to respond but forced to wait as he hacked up phlegm from the deep recesses of his lungs and spit brown liquid to the street, a second member of the group proceeded to take another drag from the unfiltered cigarette as he mumbled, "At least we enjoyed the beer, what enjoyment do they have?"

A third gentlemen holding the wall in place on a Sunday afternoon snickered, "Not only were they foolish enough to purchase such an expensive doll but how stupid to think no one would steal the damn thing."

Each of the men waved as Pastor Fischer rolled down Main Street on his way out of town. Emil had not actually heard their comments, nor had he heard the laughter but when he saw them nod their heads and slap each other on the back he knew; he knew they were making sport of the situation. He also knew that within less than thirty minutes those snickers he didn't hear would be replaced by sadness and heartache as he sat with David's family making funeral preparations.

By late Sunday afternoon, the whispers began to evaporate and the community began to take the theft seriously. "Who?" Like a sick lonely owl calling for its missing mate, was heard over and over. "Who? Who? Who?"

Indeed, who would do such a thing? The thoughts turned sober, "What type of person would steal from the church?"

On Monday evening, the men, who, similar to a well-trained Spanish dancing horse, pounded the sidewalk to assure themselves that their frozen toes still had feeling, lined the bar at the Rathskeller. The numbness that tingled in their toes progressed upward to their butts that had not slid off their barstools for nearly four hours – aside from a quick trip to the restroom to empty their bladders and make more room for another round of Hamm's. It didn't matter if one entered the stylish Rathskeller or one of the other three bars in town, the wisdom, the suggestion of who had stolen the baby Jesus, was the same. No one really believed it was possible, yet the rhetoric reflected the fear that captured men of every age. There were the men who served in WWII and fought to keep the world free from Nazism and there were the men who served in Korea and fought to keep the world free from Communism. The explanation, the only explanation that hung in the air thicker than the smoke, was "a foreigner." Only a foreigner would do such a thing. By the time the bell clanged to signal last call, the aging warriors were convinced that everything that made this country great: mom, apple pie, freedom, and the baby Jesus, was being threatened by liberal thoughts and worse yet, freedom of expression.

As the men, intoxicated with alcohol and patriotism, wobbled and stumbled from the barstool to the seat of their cars, a list of possible suspects had emerged. They had identified individuals by their station in life, by their vocation or lack thereof, and of course, some by name. And the Tuesday morning breakfast crowd, whose clothing carried the stench of grease from the two cafés, nodded their heads in agreement with the wisdom pontificated the previous evening.

The hobos, a transient crowd of men who rolled in and out of the valley as the train made a trip to the east in the morning and another west in the evening, were easy targets. Although, for the most part, they stayed to themselves and did not wander about Germantown. The city council, at least once every quarter, was directed by the mayor and concerned city folk to "clean up" the issue. Implying that a triad of hobos were responsible for the absence of the baby Jesus, would only strengthen the efforts to clean up the depot and the surrounding area regardless if there was evidence to support the allegations or not.

The sounds of David's funeral on Wednesday were the only thing that interrupted and silenced the wild speculations and accusations about baby Jesus. Pastor Fischer had prophesied correctly, the number of people who attended David's funeral exceeded old Doc Stratmann's funeral.

With both hands firmly clutching the pulpit Pastor Fischer invited the congregation to join him in a word of prayer. Following the Amen, until he delivered the opening sentence of the sermon, the entire valley held its breath. Everyone, those in the church and those unable to make it to town because the wind blew as it had done the night when David took his final breath, everyone wanted to know, could Pastor Fischer, *would* Pastor Fischer, speak the truth surrounding David's death? Could he, would he, be able to offer a word of comfort and hope?

Tuesday evening, as Emil sat alone in the church office putting the final touches on the funeral sermon, he hoped that David might once again come and speak. But, although Emil was tired, he couldn't sleep and therefore he couldn't dream, and David's voice couldn't be heard.

Without letting go of the sides of the pulpit, Pastor Fischer stared at the white embroidered funeral pall draped across David's casket. The action sent a nervous ripple through the congregation for fear the pastor might break down before he even started. What the people didn't realize was that Pastor Fischer was assuring David that he would speak the truth.

Tilting his head up, Emil surveyed the entire congregation before uttering, *"Sometimes things are never quite what they appear to be. They are never quite what we construct them to be."* He paused to let the words penetrate not only the mind, but the heart and soul of his hearers. The next sentence he delivered with more force and authority.

"In our need to control life, we concoct stories that make sense and fit the definitions of life as we determine what life should be – or, what seems reasonable and right."

Again, he paused. Without looking down at the page he continued, *"But then God comes along and disturbs our stories, disturbs our lives by entering into life. And God says, 'Sorry, but that logic, that reasoning, doesn't work. It doesn't work because I won't be limited by the absence of faith.'"*

Gasps echoed through the building, people couched nervously.

Ignoring the congregation's uncomfortableness with his words, he plowed on. *"Simply because something defies our ability to explain it, doesn't make it false. Take the birth of Jesus...How is it that a virgin can give birth? How is it that the babe in Elizabeth's womb leaped for joy as Mary drew near? How is it that Joseph was able to remain at the side of Mary? How is it that Herod, threatened by the birth of a baby, couldn't locate one peasant child and have him killed? How is it that a young man lost control of his car and we assemble today to give thanks for his life? How is it that his parents, his family, and yes, his girlfriend, can have the strength to forge on? How is this possible when logic and reason would suggest otherwise? It is a miracle."*

Every eye and ear were focused on the man in the pulpit, if for no other reason than to learn where this so-called sermon would end. The attention of people was not necessarily a sign of approval, but horror.

"Again, God speaks, 'I won't be limited by the absence of faith and therefore I will give you faith to believe that

which you can't understand. I give you the faith to forge on – because you see, not a single star in Heaven falls without my knowledge. Not one single star!'"

Leaning back slightly, Pastor Fischer released his grip of the pulpit. He looked down for the first time at the pages of the sermon, but the words were a blur. In that moment, he grasped what it meant to be the mouthpiece of God. The words were not his, but God's. Covering his mouth, he cleared his throat, took a long sip of water, stepped forward and continued.

"So, it is – that today I, God, come to you just as I came to Mary and said, 'Be not afraid', so I come and say to you, 'Be not afraid.' And just as I came to David in the waters of his baptism to claim him – to give him new life – to give him the promise of a future that never ends, so I come to you and bestow upon you the same promise."

A second time, Pastor Fischer paused and pushed his body back. This time he permitted his eyes to lock upon David's parents and his betrothed, Vanessa. After a partial smile and a nod, he scanned the rest of the congregation before continuing.

"Through the miracle of one born in a manger, nailed to a cross, and freed from the bondage of death and the cold damp tomb, so we, so you are freed to live! And so, it is that we celebrate David's life not fully understanding why, yet trusting, believing that just as eternal life is his, so too it is ours."

Before Pastor's Fischer's bottom made contact with the chair, mumbling rippled through the church.

"Who does he think he is, speaking as though he was God?"

"What kind of funeral sermon was that? He didn't talk about David once!"

"What was that smile and nod about?"

"Did you notice how he included Vanessa in his message? I bet that doesn't sit well with David's parents."

As Emil heard bits and pieces of the rumbling beneath the singing of the hymn, "What Child Is This," he could only recite the opening prayer to the sermon again, "May the words of my mouth and the meditations of our hearts be acceptable in your sight, O Lord. Amen."

It had to happen. The surprise was that it didn't occur until Thursday. Everyone in the valley knew it was only a matter of time before their names were spoken but no one wanted to be the first to publicly connect the boys to the missing figurine. Isaac and Joshua Goldman. No one will admit who initially uttered their names, but it didn't take long before the names crossed the lips of everyone in town.

Isaac and Joshua, sons of Detric, were members of the only Jewish family, Orthodox Jews no less, in Germantown. No one completely understood what brought the Goldman's to the valley. Detric, by trade, was a skilled leather craftsman, still people questioned, why the valley? There wasn't a synagogue or another Jewish family within one hundred miles.

The only justification to suspect Isaac and Joshua as guilty of stealing the baby Jesus was their religion. Those long locks, known as Payot, twisted and curled at the side of their faces, made people uncomfortable. Their refusal to work from sunset on Friday until sunset on Saturday was unnerving. Conceivably, the greatest offense was their refusal to participate in the Christmas spirit.

Detric's shop never displayed any Christmas lights or a wreath, and there was never any Christmas music. In school, the boys stepped aside at the choir concert when the choir performed a Christmas carol and they left the classroom when gifts were exchanged between classmates. Therefore, it made sense, for who, who, who else would want to sabotage Christmas?

The anti-Semitism was more than Emil could tolerate. The unjust manner by which the city preceded invoked memories of reading the disturbing words Martin Luther wrote about the Jews and later would be used by Hitler to defend his hellish actions. As much as Emil was a student of Martin Luther, there were no words to explain Luther's hatred of the Jews. Luther's sole conviction to Jesus as the Christ did not justify his abhorrence for fellow human beings. Emil was sickened as he listened to people condemn the Goldman boys as guilty simply because they were Jewish. He could not understand how the people could overlook the truth that these boys had never been in trouble with the law, unlike the Dahmen boys.

Although the Dahmen boys fit the profile as possible suspects they were ignored by most of the folks – but not necessarily Sheriff Schuette. From the moment the twin boys stepped foot outside, or were shoved out the front door and told to play somewhere other than the house, the sheriff's office spent more time with the boys than either their mom or dad. The joke was that when mom or dad couldn't tell the boys apart they called the Sheriff's office to identify who was Bradley and who was Blake.

The Dahmen boys terrorized other kids in town. They frustrated the elderly who lived alone. The entire town served as their playground. Gardens became their sandbox and flowerbeds were perfect sites to camouflage their presence as they pretended to be warriors. Sidewalks were racetracks for their bicycles stocked with playing cards clothes-pinned to the spokes. Dares were a great source of entertainment regardless if people were home. Dogs could always be teased. Chalk added "colorful" words and "creative" artistic designs to buildings around town.

The day finally arrived, the day law enforcement had prayed would never happen. The Dahmen boys both passed their driver's tests. The story, as it was told in the months following that day, is that it was Bradley who first took and passed the exam and who then turned around and took the test a second time passing as Blake. Teachers were united in saying it would have been difficult, if not impossible, for Blake to pass the test on the first attempt. But he did, and he not only passed, he scored higher than Bradley.

By the evening of that memorable day, the roar of a 1932 Ford Roadster replaced the whirring of their bikes.

The reason no one other than Sheriff Schuette suspected the Dahmen boys of stealing the baby Jesus was because they had not uttered a word about the feat. Everyone assumed the boys would be unable to keep their mouths shut if they had stolen the figurine. Sheriff Schuette, however, wasn't about to stake his reputation on an assumption. He wasn't so sure that the outcome of the boys' last court appearance had done little more than teach them to be more careful.

What everyone forgot after sixteen plus years was the reason why Joe Dahmen wanted nothing to do with the boys and why the boys labored in vain to impress their "dad." The sorted details were not necessary to comprehend the situation, only the dates. The boys were born in February of 1946, two months after Joe had returned from the Pacific Rim where he had been stationed for the past sixteen months. It might have been easier for Bradley and Blake if their mom had told them the truth but instead, they kept the secret and the boys were left wondering why they couldn't earn their "dad's" love.

Sheriff Schuette confessed to Emil that he felt sorry for the boys and that he could understand why they acted the way they did. It didn't excuse their behavior, but it did add evidence as to why children were not a part of Al's future plans.

When Isaac and Joshua were the only high school students not in attendance at David's funeral, people had all the evidence they needed to publicly convict the Goldman boys of stealing the baby Jesus. When the sheriff refused to visit the Goldman home and interrogate the boys, the town's people, including the majority of First Lutheran Church council members, demanded his resignation.

It was Detric who, before the end of the day on Thursday, called the Sheriff's office and invited Sheriff Schuette to search his home and business. When neither the figurine nor any evidence to suggest the boys had stolen the baby Jesus was found, many people from the valley continued to speculate, "Well, what can you expect? They had plenty of time to dispose of the evidence. Who, who would knowingly invite law enforcement to search one's home with the evidence available? They are Jews after all, cunning, deceiving..."

The extended silence on Friday afternoon was confusing. It was also a welcome relief to the noise Emil had heard throughout the week and the faces he saw accompanying the noise. With his eyes closed, he allowed himself to lean back in the chair and eventually gave permission for the question that had been haunting him the entire week to entertain his attention. Was First Lutheran Church and Germantown the good fit he initially thought? Was this the appropriate place for him? Could he fully...

"Pastor Fischer?"

In the state of contemplation, he had not heard anyone enter the church and climb the stairs to the office. He wondered how long someone had been standing at the office door before speaking? He wondered how long his eyes had been shut? He wondered...

"Pastor Fischer?"

He knew to whom the voice belonged without opening his eyes. He saw the face clearly in his mind. This was not the noise or the face he desired to hear and see late Friday afternoon.

"Pastor Fischer, we need to talk!"

CHAPTER 8

The legs of the chair ripped into the top layer of wax as it was dragged across the room and placed squarely in front of the pastor's desk. The pleading from the wooden floor muffled the visitor's voice as he continued to speak.

"Pastor Fischer, we need to talk. My phone has been ringing non-stop since late Wednesday afternoon. That so-called funeral sermon you delivered angered a lot of people. And of course, as church president, they are calling asking me to do something about it."

Emil sat with his elbows on his desktop and his chin resting against the thumbs of his folded hands and he listened intently to every word. When Jerome was finished speaking, Emil waited several seconds before carefully responding.

"Well Jerome, I am sincerely sorry for any inconvenience I have caused you. But..." The words hung in the air before he continued, "I'm wondering if any of those phone calls came from either the Arendt or the Hillman families?"

"Ah, well...you see..." Jerome stuttered several times without being able to complete an entire sentence. "You see, it's like...How can I best..." Finally, he just answered the question. "No. None of the calls came from either family."

Regaining his sense of purpose for coming to the church, the volume and force of his words increased. "But that doesn't mean that people are not upset with what you said."

"And just actually what are people upset about?"

"Well, let me see." Jerome unzipped his coat and pulled from his shirt pocket a crumpled, poorly folded piece of paper from which he prepared to read. "Of course, I won't mention any names…"

"No, of course not." The reply was sharp and nippy causing Jerome to stop for a moment and contemplate what Pastor Fischer might have meant. Ironing the wrinkles from the paper with the palm of his hand against his thigh, Jerome preceded with the list of complaints.

Again, Pastor Fischer sat quietly listening to every concern, every quibble, and every objection. It came as no surprise that he could attach a face or two with each complaint. After some three or four minutes of reading, Jerome stopped and looked directly at the pastor, waiting for a rebuttal, or for him to defend himself against these claims.

Instead, Pastor Fischer went down a different road. "Preaching isn't about pleasing the hearer. Many people walked away from Jesus because his words were too difficult. Many didn't like what they heard when Jesus spoke because it challenged them or revealed a deep secret they hoped to keep concealed. Let me ask you, Jerome, what is it that is bothering you?"

Jerome rolled the piece of paper between his fingers and answered cautiously, "You had the ears of the entire high school. You could have spoken of the ills of drink, drugs, and suicide. The kids and the parents want to know if David killed himself."

"You're probably right Jerome, you are probably right." As his head shook, Pastor Fischer again surprised Jerome as he continued, "But I think there is more here than Wednesday's sermon. You haven't been yourself for the past two months. You seem tense and at times distant, is there something else going on?"

Jerome pressed back, lifting the front legs of his chair off the floor and creating more distance between himself and the pastor, he questioned if Pastor Fischer knew more than he was letting on or if he was he merely concerned? Determining it was the latter, he answered, "With all that stuff happening in Cuba, who has been acting normal? Plus, you know, every marriage has its moments and, well…" he shrugged his shoulders, "it's one of those times. It will be fine though."

Before Pastor Fischer could respond, Jerome rose to his feet and returned to the issue that brought him to the church. "I just wanted you to know that people are upset with the funeral sermon." After a long pause, uncertain what else to say he concluded, "It's late and I better get going."

The two men shook hands. Jerome left the church as quietly as he had entered. Emil was left baffled. He was unable to ascertain the true motive behind that visit. He honestly couldn't determine if Jerome had something he wanted to share, possibly even confess, or if Jerome was probing to learn if he possessed knowledge about something, possibly a dark secret. He was too tired to think - it literally hurt his head. It had been an exhausting week and it was time to head home and relax.

CHAPTER 9

Emil laid in bed wide-awake at 3:30 in the morning while Katie was deep asleep beside him. It didn't seem fair that she should rest so peacefully while sleep avoided him, but he knew it wasn't her fault that his thoughts raced.

Emil stumbled to the kitchen for a snack, justified as a method to help him sleep. He popped a piece of bread into their chrome toaster, a wedding present from an aunt and uncle. The toaster hummed and the coils turned bright red, toasting the bread to a charcoal color and texture. He scaled a butter knife across the top and ate in silence.

Shuffling from the kitchen, through the dining room, towards the stairs in the dark he fought the urge to veer right and go to the den. The temptation to plop into the easy chair with a book in hand was alluring. More often than he cared to admit, he awoke in the morning with a stiff neck and aching back having fallen asleep while reading. The truth was, there was sleep and then there was *sleep*. One could sleep only to awaken in the morning feeling more tired than when one retired in the evening. Emil didn't need that type of sleep. His body, his mind needed to be refreshed and rejuvenated.

Carefully pulling the covers over his body so as not to wake Katie, his mind continued to journey across the broad landscape of his past. He couldn't connect the dots to understand why the words flashed before him but there they were. "What you do in the dark is who you are in the light." The words actually originated with Professor Forde. It sounded like a great theme for the first couple of weeks in Advent but not for the upcoming Sunday. He needed time to process and fully develop what the words meant for First Lutheran Church and Germantown. Besides, he had completed Sunday's sermon and, even if he did say so himself, it was good, not perfect, but good.

The tiny wooden bird perched on an equally tiny wooden dowel cuckooed once to signal it was half past the hour. Four-thirty and still awake, he needed to get some sleep.

His hand landed heavily upon the alarm clock. It took Emil several seconds to orientate himself and realize that he made it back to the comforts of the bed and that it was 6:30 a.m. The aroma of coffee mingled with bacon tickled the hairs in his nose and he knew that he didn't need to reach out to determine if Katie was still in bed.

It was December first today, which meant it was the day of the lighting of the city center.

Wiping the yellow remains of his sunny side up eggs with his already soggy, limp toast, Emil envisioned how he might successfully undertake the task of performing multiple roles. In addition to making sure sufficient glass bulbs were available during the decorating of the Christmas tree; assisting children as they lined up for the kiddy parade and offering the community prayer at the lighting of the Christmas tree, Katie suggested that the day's events would be a great opportunity to listen if anyone was speaking about the baby Jesus. He wanted to object, every ounce of his body screamed, "No, I'm a Pastor, not a PI." But of course, as he frequently had to admit, once again, she was right.

Bundled beneath several layers of clothes, armed with a thermos of coffee, he set off to meet up with the Kris Kringle Planning Committee on Main Street. But before he could pull the keys from the ignition of his car, he was startled.

CHAPTER 10

The crowd assembled at the 105-year-old, historic landmark stone structure fire station was larger than Emil anticipated. More disconcerting was the fact that the people were huddled in groups of five and six and no one appeared to be working - they were all chatting.

As he reached for the door handle, Emil jerked back against the upholstered seat, startled by the face pressed against his side window. At first he couldn't tell who it was through the frosted glass, but eventually, as Emil pushed his way out of the car, he recognized Walter's voice, "Vollmer's . . . and . . . bury."

"Slow down, slow down," Emil said. "Take a breath and say that again."

"Yes, yes. Sorry." Walter visibly inhaled, driving his chest outward as he took one step and then a second away from the car. "Sometime during the night or early in the morning, Vollmer's Grocery Store was robbed."

"Was anyone hurt?"

"Hurt?" It was clear Walter never considered the possibility that someone might be in the store or on the street. Unable to make sense of the question, Walter got to his main concern, "You don't suppose this could have been done by the same person who stole Jesus, do you?"

Emil hadn't had time to digest the entire event and was inclined to say, "No." Instead he offered, "It's too early to know."

Each group of people was abuzz with varying levels of speculation about whom, how, when and even why Vollmer's was robbed. This sort of thing didn't happen in Germantown nor was it supposed to happen anywhere.

As Emil snaked his way through the piles of people, greeting each person by name, he kept an eye peeled for Vernon Korkelmeier, the Kris Kringle Coordinator. Vernon was the one person he was sure was equally concerned by the lack of preparation.

When Vernon finally passed through the front door of the station and onto the street, his arrival was accompanied by mammoth snowflakes. Emil thought it was one of those moments that should be captured on camera because trailing Vernon was a stream of smoke so thick a witness might be moved to call the fire department. The irony brought a momentary smile to Emil.

The facade of Vernon's calmness debunked the moment Emil observed that he was about to lite another cigarette with the half-smoked cigarette he removed from his own lips. In spite of a steady hand and demeanor that exuded calmness, Emil knew this was nothing more than years of training and practice as a mortician. The tell was Vernon's right foot tapping out his tension.

Standing next to Vernon, keeping his eyes focused on the crowd, Emil said, "I suppose it's about time we get to the task at hand."

"Pastor, I've tried three times. You can see the results of my efforts." Vernon swung his right arm towards the crowd to emphasize his failure.

Emil enjoyed spending time with Vernon because he carefully selected his words and more often than not, brought a smile to his face.

Vernon continued, "Perhaps you might be more persuasive."

"I don't know Vern. If they won't listen to the undertaker . . ."

"Funeral home director, thank you very much."

Emil knew that would bring a smile to Vern's tight face. They both welcomed opportunities to prod one another. As outsiders to the Germantown community, the two instantly developed a bond of causal friendship. For Emil it was a different friendship than he had with the Sheriff. Vernon never visited Emil and Katie's home for social gatherings. The two seldom shared family details or other personal items and yet, as they spoke about life in the German Ghetto there existed a way of speaking that was not present with others.

"As I was saying, if they won't listen to the undertaker why would they listen to the preacher?"

Vernon wasted no time in responding, "My repertoire only consists of a soothing compassionate voice while you have in your arsenal that fire and brimstone voice. You can put the fear of God in people, and that's probably what it will take to get these people moving."

Emil wanted to thank Vernon for the gracious way he handled David's funeral and all the accommodations he made - but there would always be time for that another day. Right now these people needed to get to work.

The words sliced through the snow and redirecting the crowd of gossipers. Emil himself was startled.

"PEOPLE, PEOPLE, Listen!" Attention shifted towards Emil and he stood like a deer caught in the headlights of an oncoming car. His mouth was open, prepared to speak, but the words didn't come from him. "It is time to disperse and get to work! The forecast doesn't sound promising and the snow is already piling up. More than likely the day will be cut short along with the festivities so let's accomplish as much as we can."

The people scattered like school yard children fleeing the principal. Behind Emil's right shoulder stood Sheriff Al Schuette, who greeted Emil with a coy smile and a single nod of his head.

"Thought we better get started if we hope to get the lights on the city Christmas tree and get the parade details covered."

"Vernon and I were just discussing this every issue," Emil replied.

"Have Santa's reindeer arrived?"

"Haven't see or smelled them yet."

"Very funny. I would imagine that old man Klukas will arrive early to make sure he gets them here before the roads become impassible.

"It would make more sense if he brought the draft horses and sleigh and after the parade let the horses find their way home."

Pulling the collar of his coat up to shield his neck from the blowing snow, the Sheriff laughed, "Yeah, it would but, you gotta remember, we are talking about old man Klukas. This is the one day his reindeer are the center of attention."

Waving Vernon over to join the conversation, Emil questioned how best to restructure the day's events. "Any ideas how we should proceed and how to get the word out to folks?"

"From a law enforcement perspective I don't want country folk in town any longer than necessary. Otherwise plan to open up the fire hall to bed people down for the night. This storm could blow for days."

Lighting another cigarette before he spoke, Vernon inhaled deeply as though the smoke and nicotine held the answer. "We run the parade with whoever shows up. As usual, ending with Santa stopping at the center of the city, next to the Christmas tree where he flips the switch, and then tells the people the rest of the festivities have been cancelled."

As the three men turned to commence with the plan, Emil grabbed Al's forearm. He respected the Sheriff's job and loyalty to the office, so he would never publicly inquire about a case but in private the two men often discussed sensitive matters.

"Vollmer's, any leads?"

"You mean connections to the manger stealing."

Emil thought for a moment. "Not the purpose for my question, but, since you brought it up…"

"I'm pretty sure I know who did this one. But I need another piece of information before I interrogate the suspect. We'll talk later, too many ears here."

As Al stepped away, Walter pressed against Emil's side. "Any connection between the robbery last night and the kidnapping of the baby Jesus?" It was the first time anyone directly referred to the stealing of the figurine as a kidnapping in the pastor's presence. He had heard the rumblings, but it was always framed as humor.

Rather than commit to anything, Emil responded with a question. "What do you think, might there be a connection?"

"Times are hard Pastor, it is Christmas and all. A few extra bucks might bring a smile to a few faces?"

Walter's response took Emil's breath away for a moment, the last thing he wanted to consider was that Walter was behind either of these crimes, but... truth was, desperate people do desperate things.

Less than a third of the hundred units scheduled to march in the Kris Kringle parade even made it to Germantown, but those that did, carried the spirit of joy and peace and good will to all people. Of course, such a greeting was not intended to include the Russians or the Cubans. Santa, pulled by six reindeer, eventually arrived at the tree where he connected the extension cords and the massive eighteen-foot spruce was lit and everyone was told to go home. The only people who benefited from another snowstorm were the owners of the four bars in town. There was standing room only.

Standing next to Vern, invading his personal space with his favorite bottle of Shell's beer in hand, Emil expressed his relief that the day wasn't a total bomb. The word just left his lips when someone whispered in Emil's ear, "Did I hear someone say, 'bomb'?"

Sheriff Schuette made his way across the bar without either Vernon or Emil aware of his presence. Before Emil could explain the context of his comment the Sheriff continued, "I am about to make an arrest in the Vollmer robbery and I think you might want to tag along."

CHAPTER 11

Sheriff Schuette frequently called upon Pastor Fischer to accompany him during official county duties. On some occasions Emil's presence was requested because the person with whom the Sheriff was dealing with was a member of First Lutheran. On other occasions the task of the Sheriff was to be the bearer of bad news. And, sometimes, not knowing what was on the other side of the door it just made sense to have the pastor's collar visible to add a sense of peace to the scene. It wasn't until the two were outside the Rathskeller that Emil would learn why, specifically, his presence was implored.

"Safe to assume with the storm we're not leaving town?"

"In this business you don't want to assume anything, you know that Pastor." From here on out, until the official duties of the county were performed, Sheriff Schuette would only refer to Emil as Pastor or Pastor Fischer and demanded the same level of professionalism in return.

"So we are leaving town?"

"Didn't say that, did I?"

Reaching for the door handle, already fatigued from pushing his way through nearly a foot of snow, Emil demanded specifics.

"Get in and I will explain on the way."

The Sheriff was 99.9% confident that there was not a link between the Vollmer robbery and the missing baby Jesus. The robbery was an act of desperation and although he conceded that the stealing of the figurine might also contain a degree of desperation, it was totally different. As the Sheriff described it, "Vollmer's was about money, plain and simple. The figurine is a whole other matter. More complex if you will."

"How so?"

"The person who stole the baby Jesus is desperate but not for financial gain, for attention. It's more about making a statement."

"You mean, a religious or political statement?"

"No." The Sheriff paused as he searched for the road beneath the tires of the squad car and for the right words to describe what he was thinking. "No, I think the person who took the figurine is trying to make a personal statement."

"You sound as though you know who did it. Do you?"

"I have an idea and before you ask, it's only a feeling and respect my decision not to share any names."

"In other words, you're pretty sure it's someone in the church?"

"Yep, that I am."

The pastor wasn't sure what was more challenging, seeing the end of the car hood or fathoming the idea that someone within the church would steal the baby Jesus, in an effort to make a personal statement. If the Sheriff was correct, was this a statement against the church, against him, against . . . he could barely permit himself to think it, against God?

He shook his head and got himself back on track, preparing himself for whatever it was they were about to do. "So, the Vollmer robbery."

"Yes. The list of suspects narrowed quickly once it was revealed that the cash for the week had not been deposited as normal yesterday afternoon. Rather than question each of the suspects I focused the investigation on individuals who I feel like are in financial situations that may push them to take such a risk."

As the sheriff spoke all Emil could think about was Walter's comment and with his hands folded he prayed that he would not somehow portray his thoughts to Al.

"One name surfaced immediately...Dempewolf."

Emil nearly gave himself whiplash turning to look at the Sheriff. "Stanley, you mean, Stanley Dempewolf broke into the grocery store and robbed it? Of course, it makes sense. Stanley hasn't been in a good place for quite some time – what does he have to lose?"

"I only wish. No, it wasn't Stanley. In fact, I am sure at the time the money was stolen Stanley was passed out on the living room couch or hunched over the steering wheel of his car. No, the person who committed this crime was Thom, Thom Dempewolf."

"But, but, Thom is just a kid."

"His age might suggest he is just a kid, but life experiences have forced him to grow old sooner. Thom has been managing the lumberyard for some time and he knows they are short revenue every month. Stanley's drinking has ruined a thriving business."

"How did Thom know about the deposit being in the

store? There's another accomplice – someone who knew of Dempewolf's situation and didn't need the money themselves, yes?"

"Correct."

"Who?"

"Word on the street is that Thom has been dating Debra Vollmer for about two months."

"You mean, Debra told Thom about the money?"

"It's a little more than that, Debra was the one who was supposed to make the deposit. She said she totally forgot. Convenient, right?"

"So, where are we going first?"

"Dempewolf's"

The Dempewolf's country estates, dubbed by the town folk as the mansion in the sky, perched in bluffs overlooking the river, the valley, and Germantown. In the winter, when the trees had shed their leaves, the massive three-story log structure was visible from the city and always fueled comments; "Money can't buy happiness," "That's as close to Heaven as that family will ever get." The other three seasons of the year the house was encased by oak, elm, and birch trees shielding it from such interrogation.

The 61 Ford Galaxie "Police Interceptor" functioned more as a snow plow than a law enforcement vehicle as they scaled the driveway. It became apparent that this was not Sheriff Schuette's first excursion up the gravel road as he knew precisely the moment to drift left or right as the driveway wound a path through the dense grove of trees.

Greta, seeing Sheriff Schuette and Pastor Fischer standing on her front steps, assumed that something happened to Stanley. "Is he okay? Did he wrap his car around a tree? Don't tell me he's dead."

"Greta, Greta, stop." Pastor Fischer stepped in front of the Sheriff and ushered Greta back into the house. "Greta, we are not here about Stanley."

"Oh, Pastor, you don't know how this has been my worst nightmare, seeing you and the Sheriff standing together bearing the news that Stanley is in the hospital or dead . . ." she choked on the word before continuing, "due to being drunk." Gaining her composure, she invited them inside and asked if they would like some coffee until it hit her; this was not the most opportune time for a social call. "If, if," she stuttered attempting to find the correct words, "this is not about Stan…why are you here?"

It was Sheriff Schuette's turn to take the lead. "Greta, we're here to speak with Thom. Is he home?"

"Yes, he came home several hours ago, said the festivities were all cancelled. He said he tried to get Stanley to follow him home but . . ."

"Greta, could you call Thom." With his hat in hand the Sheriff was as direct as possible without being rude.

"Yes, sorry Sheriff. I'll go get him, I believe he's downstairs."

Before leaving the foyer, Greta stopped and turned, "Sheriff, what is this about? Is Thom in some kind of trouble?"

"I can't answer that until I can speak with him."

Pastor Fischer offered his assistance. "Greta, would you like me to go with you to get Thom?"

"Oh, no, no, I can get him, I was just wondering what this was about. You know, Thom is a good kid, but he works too much at the lumberyard. Gentlemen, why don't you follow me into the sitting room and I'll get him."

As they waited in the sitting room, both the Sheriff and the Pastor noticed the sparse décor. Scanning the first floor, Pastor Fischer became aware of the unfinished nature of the house. He couldn't help but comment, "You think the whole house is like this?"

"My guess would be, yes. I have never been past this room, but something tells me nothing is completely finished."

"I suppose it's not unlike the plumber, farrier, mechanic etc., at the end of the day the last thing they want to do is more of the same."

"Is that true for preacher's too?"

"Why do you suppose they always talk about PK's - preacher's kids?"

"Mom said you wanted to ask me some questions." Thom stood a half a step behind Greta, literally under her shadow.

"Hi Thom. Thanks for meeting with us." Both the Sheriff and the Pastor rose and shook Thom's hand forcing him to move around Greta and stand on his own.

"Yeah, sure. So, what's this about?" His handshake was weak and uninviting. The Sheriff noted that Thom's hand was already sweaty.

Pastor Fischer, wanting to help Thom feel a little less threatened, invited him to have a seat. He realized that it would be more difficult to leave the room once he was seated, as opposed to standing, when the Sheriff started to press him for a confession.

"Thom, I'll be honest with you, we're here about the Vollmer robbery."

Greta crossed the room and took a partial seat on the edge of the chair next to her son. "I heard about that. That has to be just awful for the Vollmer's. I can't imagine losing a week's worth of income."

"Greta, because Thom is a minor you may stay but I need you to refrain from commenting."

"Yes, Sheriff, I understand." Greta settled back in the only chair that remained in the room until the full weight of the moment hit her. She immediately slid back to the edge. "Wait, you don't think . . . No, that's not possible, Thom would never." Looking directly at her son she continued, "Thom tell them. You are a good boy." Her right hand rested on Thom's thigh having first patted his leg as though comforting a dog. "You work long hours at the lumberyard."

"Greta," the Pastor spoke softly, "we need you to be still and allow Thom to speak."

Offering an uncomfortable smile, Greta folded her hands and held her tongue but refused to rest against the back of the chair.

"Thom, I need you to tell me everything you know about the Vollmer robbery."

"I can't tell you anything because I don't know anything." Thom refused to make eye contact with either the Sheriff or Pastor Fischer.

Pastor Fischer attempted to intervene, "Thom, it is in your . . ."

Sheriff Schuette raised his hand to stop the Pastor. Directing his attention back to the suspect the Sheriff continued. "What can you tell me about Debra?"

"Debra?" Thom's head jerked up quickly, but the name was delivered slowly.

"Debra Vollmer, Thom." Pastor Fischer would contain his desire to get to the truth.

Accompanying a raised hand, Sheriff Schuette shook his head at Pastor Fischer. The message was clear, shut up.

Without additional encouragement Thom answered the Sheriff. "Her folks have the grocery store that was robbed last night. She's in my grade at school. She wants to be an actress.

"An actress, yeah?" Sheriff Schuette brought his right leg up and rested his ankle across the top of his left knee. The objective was to convey relaxation, to move from interrogation to conversation.

"Yeah." Apparently, the technique worked. Thom's shoulders relaxed and he looked directly at the Sheriff as he spoke. "She wants to star in movies."

"Is she any good, good at being an actress, that is?"

"I don't know. I've never seen her."

"How do you know she wants to be an actress?"

Thom paused momentarily to frame his answer properly. His body stiffened. Since this line of questions was coming from the Sheriff, Thom became suspicious he was being baited into a trap. "English comp."

"English comp? I don't understand." The Sheriff maintained his body position.

"We're in the same English writing class and we had to write a paper entitled, 'My Chosen Profession.' Debra wrote about wanting to become an actress and star in a Hollywood movie. I remember because Ms. Stuettsman said it costs a lot of money to make it in Hollywood."

Pastor Fischer smiled as he realized this was too much detail. He was lying or he was attempting to conceal something else. He was sure the Sheriff realized the same thing.

"A lot of money, ha? Any idea where Debra would get that kind of money?"

"I have no idea. You'll have to ask her."

Sheriff Schuette's right leg returned to the floor and he leaned forward. He smiled like a five-year-old who just discovered where the unwrapped Christmas presents were hid. When the Sheriff finally spoke, he did so with poise and an air of composure making it impossible to discern truth from fiction. "How do you know that we haven't already spoken with Debra?"

The color from Thom's face drained as his shoulders fell forward.

With a nod from the Sheriff, Pastor Fischer took his cue and asked Thom if he was okay. Thom didn't move.

Her motherly instinct on high alert, Greta leaned forward preparing to come to her son's aid. The Sheriff made eye contact with Greta and shook his head. Greta fell back, her body resembling that of her offspring. Beneath her breath she cursed her husband for not being here to support their son. He was never around to support anyone.

Pastor Fischer pulled his chair closer to Thom and asked again if he was okay.

Thom stared at his hands as he rubbed his fingers together. "What did she say?"

"Thom," the sheriff's chair didn't move but he leaned forward as far as possible, "the law doesn't allow me to share that information. What is important now is for you to tell the truth. What do you know about the Vollmer robbery?"

"What the hell is going on here?" The deep voice vibrated off the empty walls. "Why are the Sheriff and the Pastor here? Did someone die?" Stanley used the door frame as a third leg since his two were not providing him with much stability.

"Hi Stanley, I didn't hear you drive up." Pastor Fischer took the lead trying to make sure things didn't get out of control.

Guzzling the bottom third of a beer, Stanley took his time responding. "That's because I didn't drive up, the car is stuck at the end of the road." He drifted for several seconds, laboring to determine where he stood. His eyelids shot upward with the hope that increased light might increase his memory and it worked. "Why the hell are you here?" Greta, angry and frustrated, sought clarity, "At the bottom of the road or in the ditch where the car usually ends up?"

Dismissing his wife as if she never spoke, Stanley pressed for an answer. "You haven't answered, Sheriff. Why are you here?" The words of a drunk man were slow and loud.

Sheriff Schuette was of the belief that alcohol dulled a person's ability to hear more than the ability to speak, since every drunk always shouted.

"That's quite a walk in this weather. You're not frozen, are you? Frost bite?" Pastor Fischer was expressing compassion for a fellow human being.

"Pastor Fischer, why are you here with the Sheriff? I'm not in some sort of trouble, am I?"

Standing, Pastor Fischer carried his chair over to Stanley and invited him to sit.

Awkwardly, Stanley dropped into the chair, nearly tipping it over. He took a long deep breath before he spoke. "Thank you. Now tell me why are you and the Sheriff here?"

Before the Pastor could answer, Greta took the opportunity to vent her pent-up anger. "If you would come home and take an interest in your family rather than drinking you would know . . ."

Slurring his words slightly and still shouting, Stanley offered a rebuttal, "Pastor, doesn't it say in the Bible that a wife should obey her husband and hold her tongue? This wife of mine does nothing but bitch and worse yet, she withholds sex from me."

Calmly, Pastor Fischer placed a hand on Stanley's shoulder. "Stanley, that's a discussion for another day. Next week, you and Greta need to come to the office. Right now, we are here to discuss the Vollmer robbery."

Unaware that his head moved from side to side, Stanley said, "That was terrible. If that happened at the lumber yard, I don't know how we could survive. Wait?" Looking directly at the Sheriff he continued, "You don't think I had anything to do with that, do you?"

Greta, not detoured to speak her mind, said, "Stanley, will you shut up. They are here to speak with Thom."

With considerable difficulty Stanley placed his hand above his eyes to cut the glare as he scanned the room. Noticing that a human figure sat on the other side of Greta, Stanley rocked back in the chair. He squinted and rubbed his eyes to enhance his ability to focus. "Thom, Thom is that you? Do you know anything about this?"

There was no response.

"Thom, I am not going to ask you again." The threat from the old man was clear. Even though his father was drunk, Thom understood the message being delivered.

Reluctantly Thom spoke. "Debra's parents told her that if she continued with this foolish talk about acting and going to Hollywood, they would disown her."

"What the hell does that have to do with the robbery?" Stanley's face was flush. He assumed his son was stalling rather than confessing to something.

The Sheriff spoke for the first time since Stanley's arrival, "Stanley, you need to be quiet now and just listen. If you can't do that I will have to ask you to leave the room."

As though a drop of gas hit an open flame Stanley exploded. "This is my house, you can't…"

"Dad, stop it. Just sit there and let me finish." Thom rose from the chair to gain a physical advantage over his old man.

Hearing his son's voice and seeing him stand startled Stanley and he fell silent.

"Several weeks ago, Debra asked if I would help her get the funds necessary to go to Hollywood. At first I thought she was asking to borrow money. Slowly, I began to realize she was talking about stealing the money from the grocery store. Her plan was simple. The Friday it was her job to deposit the weekly money, she would let me know. We would stage a break in and take the deposit. The cover would be that she forgot to go to the bank. She would stick around for a day or two and then take off. That's why I'm surprised you've spoken with her."

The Sheriff looked at Pastor Fischer, both realized they needed to alert the State Patrol to be on the lookout for a sixteen-year girl.

Greta couldn't remain silent. Reaching out to grab his hand she begged for an answer, "Why, Thom? Why would you do such a thing?"

"Seriously, Mom, you really have to ask me that? Do you know how many times I . . ."

Thom choked on the next word. He swallowed hard before he continued. "Have thought about leaving?" He wiped the tears from his cheeks as he described Debra's situation. "This wasn't just about becoming an actress, she has been acting for years, pretending she was part of a loving family. This was about starting a new life."

The tears streaming down Greta's face matched those of her son. Stanley finally grasped what his son had just confessed and said, "What do you mean, 'thought about leaving'?"

Looking at his father, the words that followed were sharp and cutting. "I don't expect you to get it. I'm only here because I'm afraid of what would happen to mom if I left." Turning towards the Sheriff he finished his confession, "I guess we'll find out now, won't we?"

"Thom," the Sheriff's voice lost its authoritative edge and was soothing, "I'm not a judge. I have no idea what the outcome of this situation will be, but I promise you, I will make sure your entire story is put before the judge."

With Thom in the back seat, Al attempted to reach the main road to return to Germantown. The tracks from where Stanley's vehicle left the road and ended up 300 yards into the wooded hillside were no longer visible. The conversation in the squad car was non-existent. All eyes scoured the scene outside the car. Even Thom stared out the side window, helping to locate any landmarks that would help orientate the journey.

The second the front tires hit Main Street, the Sheriff sighed in relief and described how the next few minutes would unfold. Thom would be taken to the city jail until he could be transported to the county jail. The Sheriff and the Pastor would then proceed to the Vollmer's residence to determine if Debra already took flight. Even though the Vollmer's attended the Catholic Church, having Pastor Fischer along would be critical, as both men assumed the Vollmer's wouldn't take the news well concerning their daughter, compounded by the fact that she was their only child.

The discourse concerning the Vollmer's caused Thom to speak for the first time since they left the Dempewolf country estates, "You never had spoken with Debra, had you?"

Speaking to Thom, while looking at him in the rearview mirror, the Sheriff said, "If I recall correctly, I never did say we had spoken with her. I said, 'How do you know that we haven't already spoken with Debra?'"

Once Thom was securely tucked away in the city jail, Sheriff Schuette and Pastor Fischer made their way slowly down Oak Street to an already dark house. After knocking several times, lights came on in an upstairs window, followed by lights downstairs and finally the front door opened.

A startled voice spoke from behind the partially opened door, "Sheriff, Pastor, rather late to be out cruising the town, don't you think?" Mr. Vollmer added, "Especially during a snow storm."

After adamantly assuring Sheriff Schuette that Debra was in her upstairs bedroom, her parents couldn't understand the Sheriff's relentless demand to see her. Following a lengthy litany of interrogating questions for the teenager and a recap of Thom's comments concerning the robbery, everyone seated around the dining room table learned how Debra's departure from Germantown had been delayed by the snowstorm.

Mr. and Mrs. Vollmer, overwhelmed by disbelief that the daughter whom they loved unconditionally could mastermind such an event, were promised endlessly by Pastor Fischer that he would phone Father Neubarth first thing in the morning, since it would be dangerous for him to try and drive across town tonight. The Father's age, combined with his poor health, would make it criminal to invite him to travel.

To leave the Vollmer house, at least by squad car, Emil had to push the vehicle out of the drive way and onto Oak Street. Once the car was placed in second gear with the rear wheels spinning wildly, the car rocked forward and Emil hopped into the passenger seat. With Debra safely delivered to the city jail, Emil invited Al to spend the night at his house. Al refused on the grounds that he had two reports to write up and he knew Katie would have more than a few words to express. Plus, he didn't want to invade their privacy. Emil smiled as he realized that Al knew his wife well. The conversation that awaited him at home would be more challenging than his conversations with either the Dempewolf's or the Vollmer's.

CHAPTER 12

Emil leaped from the car as it was still rolling so that Al wouldn't have to stop and get stuck in the snow that was deeper than his five buckle rubbers. By the time Emil reached the trees that lined the boulevard at 805 Maple Street, his jeans were caked with snow at the rim of his rubbers. His calves tingled with numbness. The flickering light from his den was a beacon of light warning that possible danger lie ahead. Emil stopped for a moment and pondered how even an artificial light could resemble a star in Heaven guiding the way. Following a deep cleansing breath, he pushed aside the snow and stomped his feet twice before stepping through the doorway.

The first words Emil heard were, "Make sure you don't track snow through the whole house. I don't want to have to clean up after you."

Even though he couldn't see Katie seated in his den, he knew she would be in the overstuffed arm chair wearing her green robe with matching slippers. Her legs would be tucked up under her and her arms would be crossed and resting in her lap. She wouldn't look at him as he walked into the room. She wouldn't look at him when he apologized for his tardiness or when he apologized for not telling her where he was. She wouldn't look at him until she was able to verbalize her anger.

The repetition of such scenarios taught Emil it was best for him not to interrupt her or attempt to defend himself. There would be time later to explain the events of the evening.

As he lowered himself into the chair across from Katie, she began the process. "Jerome called wondering about church for tomorrow. Actually, he called three times and the last time said, 'Oh, I thought for sure Pastor would have returned home by now.' Walter called inquiring if he should shovel the sidewalks or wait until he received a call from you. Vanessa called and simply said she needed to talk to you. I assume it's something about David's death. And Liam called wondering if there might be a connection between the Vollmer robbery and the missing baby Jesus. And finally, Rozella called to report that she only ran a third of the bulletins for tomorrow." Katie paused for moment to add emphasis to the fact that these phone calls were tiresome and a burden. When she continued she left no doubt that she was not pleased with the situation. "Emil, I am not your personal secretary. People are worried about you when they call on a night like this and you're not home. Where were you? And, don't tell me it's confidential! I'm your wife."

Giving Katie a few more minutes to be upset with him, Emil waited and watched for his wife's body to soften so that when he spoke he could be sure she would hear his words.

"After the Christmas tree was lit and the remainder of the events were cancelled, Vernon and I went to Rathskeller for a drink and to console one another on how the weather altered the festivities. The plan was to play a few hands of Schafskopf and then come home."

"And you've been there all this time." The doubt was undeniable. Had Emil said yes, Katie would have called him a liar.

"I hadn't even tasted my beer when Al found me and requested my assistance."

"Emil," Katie's voice softened, and she whispered as lovers frequently do, "you're a pastor, not some law official. Why do you do this?"

"Al asked me to come along wi…"

"Al!" Katie no longer whispered. "Al this and Al that. Every time he comes asking for help you jump. What is it with Al?"

"Katie, this isn't about Al. You have said yourself you enjoy having Al around. What's this really about?"

Katie stopped herself from speaking and looked directly at her husband. It wasn't the first time she looked in his direction, but it was the first time since he arrived home that she took in his entire being. Lowering her eyes to his bare feet, still red from the cold and snow that made it to the bottom of his rubbers she said, "I'm worried. I'm scared. I'm scared for you, for us. And, I am tired of living alone."

"Alone?"

"Alone!"

Emil rose from the chair and knelt in front of Katie. He kissed her gently, first on her forehead and then her lips, and with her hand in his he invited her to join him in their bed.

CHAPTER 13

The day felt strange. Not gathering for worship, the absence of singing hymns in community and having the Gospel proclaimed in word created a void that defined every other moment.

The snow stopped sometime after three in the morning, but the wind made visibility impossible and transformed the landscape into a nuclear fallout.

After a phone call to make sure Al arrived home, Emil and Katie attempted to enjoy a quiet breakfast of pancakes, bacon, orange juice, and coffee. Unfortunately, the phone kept on ringing. Parishioners called to verify that church was cancelled even after the 10:00 a.m. start time.

Exasperated, Katie initially directed her annoyance towards those who called and then towards her husband. "What are these people calling for? They couldn't get there even if there was church. And, why would you call when it's after ten o'clock, either way you're not going to be there. Emil, why don't you say something when they call?"

"That wouldn't be very pastoral."

"Oh stop it! That's your excuse for everything. Truth is, you're doing nothing more than enabling them."

When the wind stopped howling late Monday afternoon human activity slowly dotted the town, like ants one by one crawling up to the earth's surface to inspect the terrain they knew as home. Emil wondered if indeed Katie was correct, was his behavior nothing more than enabling?

Vanessa was scheduled to see him after school, if there was school, on Tuesday. Stanley Dempewolf agreed that he and Greta needed to meet with him so they were scheduled for Wednesday. Today, there was a morning trip to the county jail and Jerome demanded a meeting to discuss how to make up for the lost revenue from Sunday. Perhaps the strangest conversation that occurred on Monday was with Walter's wife, Sarah.

Enabling, was it a bad thing???

The phone rang one minute after eight. Emil had been up for an hour and was nursing a second cup of coffee so he didn't sound half asleep or annoyed as he spoke into the receiver.

"Good morning, this is Pastor Fischer."

"Yes, good morning, Pastor. I trust you are faring well." Even though she didn't identify herself, Emil knew the caller. Sarah was always proper and direct. Small talk was never part of her repertoire.

"We are doing well. How are you?"

Her voice crackled - the wind was raging again and the wires were swaying and occasionally touching another wire.

Attempting to humor himself at Sarah's expense he employed the same decorum.

"What do I owe the honor of this phone call?"

"Without filling the ears of all those listening to our conversation, Pastor," the danger of a party line, "I wish to meet with you to speak about a particular young woman."

"Is this a conversation that can wait until later in the week?"

"No. As it is, it has to be sooner than later as things are growing."

Growing? She couldn't know. How could she? He replayed the phone conversation with Vanessa and how he had intentionally avoided any discussion about pregnancy. He remembered how he cautioned Vanessa to keep their conversation simple. Growing? Did she know something? She was, after all, David's aunt. And, if she knew something, did that also mean that she might know who the father was?

"On second thought, I agree, sooner rather than later is better. As soon as the visibility returns I'll be over." Then he added, "I still need to dig my car out from the fire station."

While Emil pulled on several layers of clothing and prepared to scale over mounds of snow drifts on his way to Sarah's house, he thought more about what Katie had said and she was right, he was enabling.

CHAPTER 14

The trek to Sarah's home, at the east end of Spruce Street, with the addition of elevation, could easily have been described as scaling Mt. Everest. The inconsistent density of the layer of crust atop the snow made it challenging to move forward with any rhythm. In spots the snow carried his weight and in other's he broke through and sunk waist deep into the snow that then quickly enclosed his body like quicksand. He was thankful that during the last snow storm he placed the scoop shovel in the trunk of his car, it would have been difficult to try to carry it with him as he navigated his way through the snow piles.

The two-story house, complete with a screened in wrap around porch, which served as home for Sarah and the kids, was the same house Sarah lived in until she married Walter. Other than the farm house it was the only place she had ever slept. The timing of her separation from Walter served her mother well as she was no longer able to live alone. Now, with Sarah in the house, she could remain home a few more years before being forced into the convalescent home.

Emil enjoyed making pastoral calls to Sarah's mom, Mrs. Arendt, as her mind was sharp. It was her body, especially her legs that refused to cooperate. He felt ashamed as he thought about Veda and how he forgot to check in with her following David's funeral. He recognized that the grandparents were frequently ignored when an untimely tragedy struck and yet, with the busyness of the season, he fell into the same trap. Being alone with his thoughts he decided to be honest with himself, as he willed himself up the steep hill, he confessed that since Sarah's return to the house he hadn't visited Veda nearly as frequently as he did previously. Veda was a phenomenal story teller. She was able to take you on a journey and over the course of an hour weave together ordinary events, including the lives of people, that might involve humorous or serious situations and ultimately deliver you full circle where you are left rejuvenated and invigorated.

Although he was on the verge of fatigue and exhaustion Emil wore a momentary smile as he thought about how Veda marveled at how different her children were, although raised in the same house. Until David's death, she chuckled at the unpredictability of life. Sarah, as reported by Veda, couldn't wait to graduate from high school. Germantown was the last place she wanted to live, well, actually, the last place she wanted to live was on a farm. To separate herself from rural values she developed a pompous attitude. David's father, Steffen, on the other hand, couldn't see himself doing anything but farming and fortunately married into a farming family complete with a dairy set up. Veda was fond of saying, "God must have a sense of humor and love to laugh, how else do you explain life?" He wondered what she would say when they met to discuss David's death.

Having successfully scaled the steep hill, Emil needed to catch his breath before he climbed the final three steps onto the porch. As his rubber boot packed the snow on the first step, Sarah swung open the door.

"Pastor, once you hear what I have learned you will agree your trip here was worth your time."

Emil thought to himself, if nothing else, Sarah is consistent.

Ushered into the living room, Emil continued to open up the layers of his clothes to let fresh air in and keep from sweating. If he didn't dry out his return trek would be chilly, even dangerous.

Comfortably seated away from the heat register, he nodded that he was ready to hear the news about what was growing. He told himself repeatedly that he would not confirm or deny anything Sarah said. If this was about Vanessa, she didn't need this to hit the public airwaves before she informed her parents.

The pompous tenor was undeniable. "I assume you know about Vanessa's condition."

"Condition? What condition would that be?"

"Oh, Pastor, don't be coy with me."

Now there was a word he hadn't heard recently.

"Sarah, farthest thing from my mind. I am not sure to what condition you refer. Her struggle to understand David's passing? Her being held responsible for the accident by some people?"

"No, I mean, the condition you have yet to name."

"Well, then your assumption is flawed because these are the issues of which I am aware."

"I don't understand. Then why did you agree to meet?"

"Because you implied the situation was critical and time was of the essence. And by the way, you never mentioned Vanessa when we spoke on the phone."

"Well, it **is** about Vanessa and since you're not aware of any other conditions, this may come as a surprise . . ." Sarah paused as though Emil needed to catch up with this train of thought. "Vanessa is with child."

Emil worked not to change his facial expression as he mentally prepared a reply.

"And how is it you know this?"

"A little birdy told me."

Emil couldn't resist the temptation, even though it was petty, to throw her own words back at her. "As you said, don't be coy." He followed up by leaning forward to accentuate his concern for such tongue wagging. "I'm . . . I'm serious. How do you know this is true? Such a rumor will only increase the poor girl's stress."

"You're saying you know she's not pregnant?"

His brow wrinkled, "I'm not saying anything, at the moment, other than to question how you know this to be the truth and to acknowledge the power of such words. Merely hinting that Vanessa *might be* pregnant could be devastating to her and her family. As a blood relative of David, I would think you would do everything to ensure Vanessa's safety." Emil sat back to let the full impact of his words settle in before he asked again, "How do you know this?"

"I cannot tell you the individual's name. I promised not to divulge their identity, but they are a reliable source."

"So reliable they can't be named." The sarcasm was so thick it clung to the walls like wallpaper paste. "Sarah, I would suggest you keep this to yourself until I can do some additional checking."

"I would agree, I . . ."

"That includes not saying anything to your children or Veda, unless of course you have already."

"Oh, God no!"

The words surprised Emil. It was the first he could recall ever hearing Sarah use a phrase that would be heard in a bar.

"The children are too young to grasp such a situation and as for mother, it would break her heart."

Now Emil was certain he needed to schedule a visit with Veda before he left the house.

Sarah was compelled to have her pastor understand her motivation. "I just thought you should be aware of the condition . . ."

"Assumed condition."

"Yes, yes, **assumed** condition, as you work with Vanessa and her family. The same would hold true for Steffen."

Emil thanked Sarah for her concern and pleaded with her not to speak of this until she heard back from him. He also asked if she was comfortable making the same request of the person who shared this news with her.

Making sure the ear flaps of his hat covered his ears and his rubbers were buckled, Emil left to dig out his car.

The only visible portion of Emil's car was the thin wire antenna. Unfortunately, the position Emil parked the car in on Saturday morning served as a perfect wall for a ten foot snow drift to rest against. After assessing the ramifications of leaving the car buried until spring, Emil began to claw at the snow at the spot he hoped was directly above the trunk. The very trunk where his one and only shovel rested peacefully. He reconsidered the wisdom of placing the shovel in the trunk.

Once the majority of the faded green trunk was exposed, Emil started trying to figure out how to thaw the lock so that the key might turn. As he pounded with his fists he heard Al's voice. "Beating on the thing won't make it start any faster."

"Not trying to start it, if I was, I would be kicking it." Together they laughed and set to work prying open the trunk.

Stopping to pull his soggy mittens back in place, Emil asked, "What are you doing here anyway? Can't be on patrol."

I called your house to see if you needed another package of venison and Katie said you were out on a pastoral call and then were going to try and dig out the car."

Emil could only smile. Katie was so frustrated with him and, yet, she was his best ally.

"Venison, ha? Sounds like cabin fever."

"Call it what you want. Do you want my help or not?"

"Shut up and dig." Emil appreciated that Al never pestered for details about his work. He never inquired about whom he visited on such a wintery night.

Beneath the stars in Heaven the two men labored endlessly, not needing to say a single word, but knowing their friendship was critical to their longevity in Germantown.

Al woke on the couch in the Fischer's living room two hours before the sun was scheduled to make an appearance. It wasn't the first night he slept on the tweed davenport rather than in the comfort of his own bed. Over the past twelve months it wasn't at all uncommon for him to sleep on Katie and Emil's couch.

Three hours after freeing the shovel from the trunk, Al and Emil returned to the house. The car was no longer buried or stuck but none of the city streets had been plowed.

As another layer of warm clothing was removed and another bottle of Shells was opened, Katie popped another kettle of popcorn. Both of the guys were exhausted and the beer muffled their screaming muscles. And the popcorn? Well, the popcorn was just plain good. Katie had a knack for making the perfect kettle of popcorn. She said it was because she never washed the oil from her hand cranked kettle popcorn popper.

The scene unfolded in basically the same manner three or four times a month; Al would repeatedly compliment Katie on her popcorn making skills and, at some point, suggest she needs to market her secret. They would all laugh, open another beer and grab another handful of popcorn and continue to share stories into the wee hours of the night.

It was such light-hearted banter like this that made Katie's comments about Al the previous day all the more much strange. She was critical of him on one level and on another welcomed and enjoyed his presence.

Without making noise, Al made himself two slices of peanut butter and grape jelly toast. He heated water in the tea kettle for a cup of instant coffee before leaving the house to walk home and get the squad car to transport Thom and Debra to the county jail.

Moments after Emil's alarm clock sounded he switched on the radio to get the latest updates. The forecast was simple; "Temperatures dropping throughout the day until reaching negative fifteen degrees. In spite of the sixteen inches of snow, school will be open, but buses will travel on plowed roads only." The announcer continued with weather related stories, but Emil had the two bits of information he needed to start his day. He needed to dress, once again, in layers when he walked to retrieve his car and school would be in session which meant Vanessa would definitely be coming to his office. It didn't matter if the bus traveled past the Hillman farm place, there would be no stopping her from driving into town.

The condition of the city streets had drastically improved thanks to the overnight plows but, less than two miles from town, Emil wondered if he should have called the Hillman's to cancel Vanessa's appointment. The inability of the snowplows to scrape the layers of compacted snow on the country roads left ruts that threatened to consume Emil's vehicle and simultaneously toss it beyond control several feet left or right. The thirty-five-minute trip warped into an hour and fifteen minute excursion.

Encased in his own prison of confinement, his arms ached, his eyes grew wary, his foot was numb, his calf tightened beyond belief, and the pinched nerve in his shoulder screamed, all activating his mind to search for a means of escape. Any option of a physical escape was senseless as it would have left him stranded on the side of road in freezing temperatures. The only feasible alternative was for his mind to take him outside the confinement of his vehicle. Ironically, where he journeyed to was, of all places, prison.

It had been several years since Emil stepped foot in the state penitentiary. He first met Markie Hines when he was assigned to the county jail to practice his pastoral skills. Each seminary student was required to complete a full year of pastor care and counseling that included volunteering in the community at one of the forgotten places. Markie was accused of murdering another man and was awaiting arraignment when Emil walked through lock up and offered counseling services to any prisoner. When Markie inquired about the chaplain services the guard stepped forward, shielded Emil from the prisoner and informed him that this prisoner was off limits. Emil politely thanked the guard for protecting him, but stepped around his two hundred plus pound frame to look at the man who requested his presence. Markie could have passed for a twelve year old boy. His thin framed stood little more than five feet five inches and his long fingers were carefully wrapped round the iron bars. Emil's inspection of the young man was cut short.

"I'm sorry preacher, but this man is too dangerous for you to get close to." The guard, with his baton drawn, pressed his massive frame between Emil and the prisoner again.

Too dangerous? Were they each referencing the same individual?

"Again, thank you for your concern, I do appreciate it, but every individual, regardless what they are accused of, has the right to a visit from a clergy person. Emil had no idea if that was true, but it sounded good and he tried to deliver the words with confidence.

"Well preacher, you should know, he is a murderer. He killed a white man."

The words "killed a white man" hung in the air, as though that was different than killing a man of color or for that matter, a woman of any color. Emil, again, stepped to the side of the guard to inspect the prisoner. "I promise, I will be careful, but why don't you stay close so if something should happen you can step in."

"That's a good idea preacher. A good idea."

As the guard shuffled to the next cell Emil moved within arm's reach of the iron bars. "What's your name son?"

"Son?" Anger spit the words back in Emil's face. "Don't call me that. You ain't my parent as I ain't got no parents. Besides, you ain't even old enough to have kids." And then as an afterthought he asked, "You sure you're a chaplain?"

"I am." Emil figured it was a safe bet that the prisoner would not be running a background check on him. Before the prisoner could challenge such a claim he asked, "What's your name?"

"They call me Markie."

"Markie it is."

"Can you get me out of here?" The anger and doubt melted from Markie's voice and the question became more of a plea.

"I can't Markie, that's a job for your lawyer. You do have a lawyer, don't you? A defense attorney?"

Markie looked at the guard and mumbled. "Yeah, I guess so."

"You're not sure if you have a lawyer?"

"Some guy came and stood behind the guard and said, 'I am your court ordered defense attorney.' He said he would read my file and ask for bail to be set, but he added that I shouldn't get my hopes up since I was black and all."

Emil turned towards the guard to confirm that Markie recalled the events correctly. The guard only smiled.

Markie continued, "I asked him if I could trust him and he said he was a defense attorney and that he worked for the people." And then he added, "What other choice do I have?"

After spending some time with Markie, Emil learned that Markie was returning from school when he heard his sister screaming for help even before he opened the front door. This guy, three times the size of his sister, was on top of her, holding her down, raping her. The guy struck her again and again in the face and told her to shut up and enjoy it. Markie described how he grabbed the only thing he could find, a baseball bat he left in the hallway from the day before, and he came up behind the guy and swung with all his might. As the guy tumbled off her, he saw his sister, naked. Her face and chest were purple from bruising and blotches of red blood were everywhere. She was unable to move, she just stared at the ceiling. He took a wash cloth and carefully removed the blood from her body and located undergarments and a dress and he methodically placed them on her as if she was a mannequin so no one else might see the filth the dead man imprinted on her body. And then he called the police.

That day Emil learned a difficult lesson. Never, never promise anyone something beyond your own control. In an effort to comfort an obviously distraught young man, innocent of murder, simply attempting to protect his sister, he told Markie, "There is no way you will be convicted of murder. You're innocent."

Markie's guilty verdict brought Emil to the state penitentiary numerous times over the years. In part because he was guilty of creating a false sense of hope and in part because he was Markie's pastor regardless what church he was serving.

Emil parked behind the county jail and crawled out of his own confinement. He pulled his jacket tight and reminded himself not to commit the same sin again with Thom. He could speak a word of forgiveness, but he couldn't grant a pardon. He could speak of strength and presence, but he couldn't promise understanding. He could speak on behalf of a heavenly judge, but he couldn't speak for an earthly judge.

Ironically, he would remind himself of similar words later in the day as he met with Vanessa.

Vanessa appeared in the doorway right on time. Even though he knew she would be arriving soon he was still startled when he looked up and saw her. Tucked next to the doorframe it appeared that she might be hoping to go unnoticed. He wondered how such an innocent girl could be with child. Maybe today would bring forth some answers.

Before he could invite her into the office she nervously stepped across the room. Her stride was short and choppy as though she didn't want to reach her destination. Standing before two chairs, one wooden and one metal, she turned and asked, "Does it matter which chair I sit in?"

He found it strange that she would inquire about the appropriateness of a chair, this wasn't her first time in his office and she had always just sat down before. There was a lot more transpiring than he could fully grasp. Stumbling over his words as he attempted to make meaning of her question he assured her it didn't matter. "No, no, take the one, which ever one is most comfortable for you."

He didn't wait for her to get comfortable before he continued to speak. Her coat clung to her left shoulder as she focused on his questions. "How are you feeling? Is everything going okay?" He could have asked more questions, but he knew full well that these questions were a prelude to the more serious questions that needed her clarification.

Her answers were short and to the point. She was feeling fine, it was still early in the pregnancy, and as far as she knew, everything was progressing okay.

Before they discussed how to go about telling her parents, the purpose for the visit, he needed to know if she had discussed her condition with anyone else.

"Who would I tell?" Her voice was heavy with disbelief.

"I don't know Vanessa, that's why I am asking. Is it possible that you didn't tell anyone, but they somehow got a clue?"

"Got a clue?" The crease deepened in her brow, she was clearly perplexed by Emil's questions. "I don't know what you're suggesting, Pastor." As she acknowledged her confusion her right hand went to her stomach again where she rubbed the fabric of her sweater with circular motions.

"Is that a natural action for you?"

She shook her head and shrugged her shoulders, "Is what a natural action?"

He nodded towards her midsection as he spoke. "Your hand on your stomach, moving so effortlessly?"

"Oh," she smiled. "I, I didn't even realize my hand was moving." Her hand immediately dropped to her side.

"We all have little ticks, things we do when stressed. In poker they called it a tell. Observing a person's body language can speak louder than a person's voice. Before you realized you were pregnant did you place your hand on your stomach?"

She thought before answering, she didn't think so.

At that point Emil proceeded to inform Vanessa of his visit with her Aunt Sarah. Initially he was sure someone told her that Vanessa was pregnant, but now, knowing how insightful Sarah was, how she missed very little, he was quite sure her conjecture was based on watching Vanessa very closely, probably during the day of the funeral. Which meant, she was fishing to confirm her suspicions.

"That makes sense why mom and dad have little to do with that witch. Before you remind me to respect my elders, that's mom's name for her."

"That doesn't mean you should use such language."

"I guess it's just a habit. You hear something enough times and pretty soon it sounds natural."

Not wanting to lose focus of the purpose for their meeting, Emil pressed Vanessa. "So, how do you go about telling your parents that you're pregnant?"

"There is no easy way. No matter what or how I say it, they'll be so disappointed."

"Are you concerned that they'll be angry with you?"

Her head shook several times before she spoke and even as the words were delivered her head continued to move. "No, not angry, not like they'll be yelling. But, more like, how could you? How did it happen? Who is . . ." She stopped herself. To complete the question would give her pastor permission to revisit an area she previously refused to answer. An area too painful to visit. An area better left buried.

It didn't matter that she didn't ask the question; Emil had planned to pursue the topic regardless. He was convinced the answer to the question would influence how Vanessa should go about sharing the news of her pregnancy. Obviously, her parents would assume David was the father, unless, unless of course . . . Emil wouldn't allow himself to fathom the possibility that . . . No, he told himself he needed to keep an open mind and allow Vanessa to share the father's name. His frustration, his quandary was, he didn't know how to simultaneously "allow" and "force" Vanessa to share something she previous vowed not to share. Was there a magical way to frame the question?

He leaned back in the chair, staring at the ceiling while his hand patted the seconds on the desk top. Six, seven, eight, his hand ceased, his head tilted forward, and his eyes met Vanessa's. "You're right. They are going to ask who the father is. Are you going to let them think it's David or will you tell them the truth? And what about David's parents? What about David?" He hated himself for going there, but she needed to consider all the consequences of her answer or her silence.

Tears streamed down her checks until the salty liquid dropped from her chin and formed two separate puddles in her lap. She sat motionless. He knew the game, the first one to speak lost and even though this wasn't a game, he wasn't about to speak first no matter how much his insides twisted and threatened to push the contents of his stomach upward.

The minute hand on his watch pounded in his ears. For the better part of ten minutes it was the loudest noise in the office. Without lifting her head, she whispered, "If I tell you, do you promise not to tell another single soul?"

Equaling the softness of her voice Emil answered, "Without knowing the name, the identity of the person, I can't promise you that. I wish I could, but I would be lying to you. And you deserve the truth."

"I mean, why does anyone else need to know?"

"I can't answer that – but I can say, for your own well-being I believe you need to share the truth about the father of this child."

There was another interlude of silence, this time only a minute or two. Folding her hands, she spoke. "I know you're right, but it's so wrong..."

"What's wrong, Vanessa?"

Before another word could be spoken by either of them, Jerome stepped into the office. "Oh, oh, I'm sorry. I didn't realize you were with someone Pastor. The, the door was open, and I thought, well, it doesn't matter what I thought. I see you are with someone. I'll leave you alone. Sorry, for interrupting."

The moment was lost. Vanessa gathered her coat and vanished from the room before Emil could step out from behind the desk. His voice was lost in the rafters as he called after her to stop and come back. A search of the church also revealed that Jerome had vacated the building.

Emil grabbed the phone and dialed the number he knew by heart. He invited Al to dinner that evening.

CHAPTER 15

Saturday evening arrived with amazing speed. The stress of the holiday season took hold and Emil barely had time to catch his breath. By the time he sat down to write his sermon at midnight, the stress he felt in his head, as it pounded with a migraine, was intensified by the fact that he had yet to write a single word and the service started in less than ten hours.

Hunkered down in the den, his fingers struck the keys of the Royal Aristocrat typewriter with speed and fluidity; he was an accomplished typist. He appreciated the typewriter, which had been a graduation gift from several members of his family, as it was a vast improvement over the 1930's Remington machine his grandfather gave him when he left for college. His appreciation for the machine did not interfere with his ability to recognize the humor in the name, Aristocrat, as he considered himself anything but. Emil readily acknowledged that he was among a small handful of people in Germantown who possessed an advanced educational degree and yet, the effectiveness of a pastor was not in separating self from others, but becoming one of the people.

His fingers froze momentarily atop the keys; he leaned back in the chair when he realized that was the message of

Christmas. God humbled himself and took on human form in order to become one of the people. The baby delivered by Mary was both fully human and fully divine. The infant nursed at Mary's breast. He needed his diapers changed. He needed to be held, cuddled, bathed, and protected. The Gospel to be read later that morning included the words of the Prophet Isaiah, "Behold, I send my messenger before thy face, who shall prepare thy way; the voice of one crying in the wilderness; Prepare the way of the Lord, make his paths straight." Who was this one of whom the prophet speaks? Was it a baby, a baby that has gone missing from the Nativity? Seriously, had the Christ child really gone missing?

Emil sprang forward in the chair, a new sheet of paper rolled into the Aristocrat. He knew what the good news was; now he was tasked with connecting that truth with his parishioners. As his fingers struck the keys the faces of those with whom he walked throughout the week began to appear. It was his job, his calling, to connect the good news to those faces. At this point in his career he was secure enough to know it didn't matter if every face was in the pews later that morning, because no matter what faces were there, they all had a story and that story was part of God's story.

Vanessa, Thom, Thom's parents, Jerome, Al, Katie – there was always Katie – she was somehow different from all the rest.

The faces came sporadically. The first to appear was the man who demanded the better part of what was now, yesterday. Emil already had delivered a sermon specifically for this gentleman and therefore he wondered if there was something he missed, something he could have said better. Elmer Trebesch died Sunday during the snow storm. Apparently, he froze to death in an attempt to locate two cows that never appeared at the barn door for the evening milking. His grandson found his body Tuesday morning resting comfortably against the base of an old oak tree. His wife told Emil that more than likely Elmer, in his stubbornness, refused to return home without the cows. She assumed he became disorientated and walked head long into the tree. Exhausted, he decided to rest in order to catch his breath and well... Emil found it of interest how in times of grief or trauma people find comfort in things that under normal situations no one would even acknowledge. Several members of Elmer's family reported how the old oak in the pasture had been a favorite location for Elmer to sit and rest in his later years.

Emil wasn't exactly sure why Elmer's face kept coming to mind, other than that, in some ways, Elmer was like Emil's grandfather. Both had been strong men, strong in so many ways but as age took its toll, they struggled to have an identity. Both struggled with the purpose and meaning of life. Both struggled to find something that would give them value. In a community where value was linked to work...

"Work? What a joke." As though on cue, Greta's words from earlier in the week screamed in Emil's head. It didn't take long before Stanley made an appearance in order to rebuff his wife with words not fit to repeat. The anger, the hatred, the pent-up hostility that flowed unabashedly between the two of them did not surprise Emil. Emil had heard other couples argue this way. What did surprise him was that when he spoke of Thom, it did little to alter the dispute. He wondered if they could remember the last time a civil conversation occurred between the two of them.

"That would be a 10-79 call." Somewhere at that moment, Al was smiling knowing that Emil finally remembered the official police call number for a domestic disturbance. Al seldom questioned Emil's motives but when he asked Al to follow Vanessa after their meeting on Tuesday evening when he came to dinner, Al asked, "What's this about?" Reluctantly Emil started with a disclaimer. "I don't have any facts, it's only a feeling, something deep within is telling me there's something terribly wrong here."

"You know I trust you Pastor..." This was now official business, it was more than a request from a friend, this was one professional speaking with another professional, "but, I need you to expound upon that feeling you have."

When Katie returned to the dining room table to finish clearing the dishes she recognized immediately that her presence was not wanted. "I'm going to wash the dishes. Do you want me to open another bottle of wine?"

Politely, Al offered to assist with dishes.

Right on cue Katie said, "No, you guys stay here and finish your conversation. When I'm done with the dishes we can play a game of Schafskopf."

Both guys could hardly contain themselves as Emil said, "Bring your coin purse you know you never win."

With Katie safely out of earshot Emil returned to Al's question. "Vanessa is pregnant."

"I'm sorry to hear that, it must be tough with David's death."

"It is and even more difficult considering David is not the father."

Al leaned forward, his elbows slid across the table top nearly knocking his wine glass over. "So . . . who . . . is the father?"

"That's just it. She refuses to tell me. Nor would David."

"You mean you knew about this before David's accident?"

Should he tell the truth about the dream and hope he wouldn't lose any credibility with Al? Or lie in order to avoid an awkward explanation? He decided on the truth and hoped a simple answer would be efficient and Al would leave it alone. "No."

"Wait a minute...you just said..."

"Yes, I know what I said." Emil proceeded to share his experience in the hospital and how it fit precisely with what Vanessa told him later. He made it clear that somethings just were beyond human logic and it simply required faith.

With his wine glass empty, Al looked Emil directly in the eye and said, "So, tell me more about this feeling. David's not the father, so are you suggesting that something is horribly wrong with how she got pregnant or with who the father is?"

"Yes."

"Yes, what? Are you saying it might be both?"

"I am saying, I don't know, but, it all feels so wrong. There is too much secrecy connected with this pregnancy."

"Her father?"

Even before he spoke his head was shaking. "I don't think so. Actually, I highly doubt it."

"Based on? I mean, we see it all too often. And you'd be surprised. Rather, let me say, you'd be sick if you knew of some of the families where we encounter this."

"I believe you, Al, but this doesn't feel like that. Either way, I am asking you to follow her, to monitor who she meets. It might reveal who the father is."

"Do her parents know?"

"That's why she came to the office today, to plan how to tell her parents. She is probably telling them right about now."

Emil mentally returned to his office and stared at the typewriter before him. He struggled to continue writing the sermon. Part of him was relieved to know that Al's investigation since Tuesday evening revealed nothing of substance while another part was frustrated. The text rang in his ears. "Prepare the way of the Lord."

His left hand covered the keys, A, S, D, F, and his right covered, J, K, L, ;, he was ready to formulate the ending of his sermon when Jerome's face appeared unannounced and apparently connected to no one. It baffled Emil as he considered why Jerome stood in the doorway and then departed without any explanation on Tuesday afternoon. A phone call on Thursday offered no answers. There was something going on with Jerome and yet for whatever reason he was unable to share it with Emil. And that provided Emil with the closing to the sermon.

"The baby, God himself, was coming whether we recognized it or not. Whether we were ready or not. Jesus would be in the manger come Christmas. Jesus would be here for you no matter what."

As Emil switched off the light on his desk he prayed that the words he delivered in five hours would be true for him as well. He needed Jesus to be there for him, and for Katie.

In the darkness of the den he realized that he didn't include Katie in his sermon. Katie never made an appearance in his mind. Cautiously he pondered what that meant.

CHAPTER 16

A degree of exasperation swirled through Emil's body, the effects of which were greater than the howling northwest wind, as he shuffled down the sidewalk towards the car after church Sunday morning. He was hunched over so badly and walking so slowly that he resembled a ninety year old man. He was stressed because hardly anyone commented on the quality of his sermon. Apparently, the only concern among the congregation was the missing baby Jesus. As he shook hands after the service, person after person asked if the figurine had been located. He wanted to shout, "The Lord is coming whether we find the figurine or not! Don't you get it?" Instead, he smiled and reported that there were no new developments.

There was only one more Sunday in Advent and Christmas Eve would arrive the very next day. Waiting for the car to warm before putting it into gear, Emil doubted his ability to prepare the people for the coming of the Christ child. He was embarrassed to admit that he found himself asking God to assist in locating the figurine. With his left hand firmly gripping the steering wheel and the right preparing to slide the gear shift lever down into first, he stopped himself. Lifting his foot from the clutch, his body dropped back against the seat. Staring inattentively through the windshield, he sensed that there was something else not right, yet he lacked the ability to name it. He even muttered to himself, "What am I missing?" He was unable to pin point it, to see whatever it was that made his insides stir.

Katie met her husband at the door. "Rozella has called three times frantically trying to find you."

"I, I was…what does she want?" There was no point in attempting to explain his tardiness, Katie would never understand. It was better simply to move on.

"She wouldn't say, but you are supposed to call the county jail the moment you walk into the house. Have you heard from Al?" There was an edge of concern in Katie's voice. "Didn't you see him in church?"

"I have not heard from Al and he wasn't in church."

"Do you think this has anything to do with Al?"

'Yeah, he probably has a lead on the figurine." He lied, something he seldom ever did with Katie, but…

"Yeah, that's probably what it is. You better call and get the good news."

Emil kept getting a busy signal at the county jail so he decided to drive there.

As he pulled into the parking lot Emil saw Father Neubarth from the Catholic Church pulling the collar of his overcoat up to shield his neck from the northwest wind.

Recognizing his colleague's vehicle, Father Neubarth stopped and waited for Emil to exit his car. Father Neubarth grabbed Emil's hand and shook it and didn't let go until they had made it across the parking lot. The wind made it difficult to discern anything Father Neubarth said other than, "Good to see you . . ."

The receptionist had been watching for them so the moment their feet hit the first step of the concrete stairs the locked door swung open.

"Welcome gentlemen, thank you for coming over so quickly. The sheriff is waiting in his office." The three of them stood in a small space trapped between two locked doors. "Give me a moment and I'll unlock the door and usher you down to his office."

Still unaware of what awaited him on the other side of the barrier, Emil turned to Father Neubarth and asked, "Do you know what this is about?"

"All I know is that there was an accident with one of the prisoners. I don't know the severity or the name of the individual."

What both clergymen noted as they moved through the outer office was the buzz and chaotic movement of personnel. Emil wondered if, on a miniscule platform, this scene mimicked what must have been occurring in the White House amongst the chiefs of staff during the early days of October. Before they reached Al's office, Emil noticed that his body temperature rose, and he mumbled, "Dear God, someone is dead. Someone from Germantown. Otherwise, why call both Father and me. Tho..."

The introduction was short and to the point. "Sheriff, the clergymen are here from Germantown."

Al's face said it all. But who? Who succeeded in taking their own life?

The sheriff waited for both men to be seated before he cleared his throat and spoke softly. "Father Neubarth,

Pastor Fischer, thank you both for coming on such short notice. I guess that's the way it is with a crisis, one does not plan or schedule them, they just happen." The wooden swivel chair creaked out a groan as Al shifted his weight. Al was clearly uncomfortable with the news he had to share. "We had an accident earlier this morning. An accident that cost a young woman her life. It is an ongoing investigation and therefore, I can't share any details with you. What I can share is that Debra Vollmer was found dead in her cell shortly before eight this morning. I have not notified the parents yet. Rather than receiving the news over the phone and having them rush here in this weather, I propose that the three of us or at least, Father Neubarth, you and I go to the Vollmer home. There is no reason for the family to come here. The coroner is finishing up his work and the body will soon be moved to the mortuary for a complete autopsy."

Father Neubarth was nodding in agreement before the Sheriff finished. "My only question is, would it be possible for the family, if they wish and I am guessing they will, to view the body before the autopsy?"

The Sheriff paused, and stared at his hands on the desk before he answered. His voice cracked for the first time, "I can appreciate their desire, but . . ." the small office filled with tension as the pause extended beyond the socially accepted interlude. He cleared his throat several times before continuing. "I would not recommend it until the funeral director has had an opportunity to fix the body."

"What are you saying, Sheriff?"

"Father, I wish I could tell you more but right now, I can't. You just need to trust me."

Emil spoke up, fearful that Father Neubarth was not about to let this go. "Whatever the two of you think is appropriate, I support. How are you doing, Sheriff?"

Speaking just to Emil, Al said, "Thanks, but that's not the issue at the moment, there will be time to discuss that later."

Father Neubarth and Emil rode in the back seat as Sheriff Schuette drove the squad car to the Vollmer home. It was the second time in a week that Pastor Fischer and Sheriff Schuette knocked on the Vollmer door and neither visit ended well.

As the squad car pulled into the parking lot of the jail, Sheriff Schuette thanked the men for their comforting words and support during such a challenging situation. As expected, the Vollmer's asked immediately to see their daughter. In tandem, Father Neubarth and Pastor Fischer condoned the requested but prayed that they might be patient and allow themselves time to prepare and for the investigation to unfold as needed. Gripping a photograph of their daughter tightly, the Vollmer's grudgingly agreed. Father Neubarth assured them he would return to their house after getting his car from the parking lot of the jail.

Before leaving the side of the squad car, Emil grabbed his friend's shoulder and pulled him close, "I will see you later tonight at my house. It doesn't matter what time you get done here, I'll wait up for you."

"Thanks, I also have an update about our other matter."

Half smiling Emil asked, "The baby has been found?"

"It has to do with the baby, but not that baby." Al didn't return Emil's smile with one of his own.

The squad car pulled into the driveway at three minutes past 12:00 a.m. Al didn't bother to knock, he just walked into the house, kicked his military style boots off next to the door, draped his coat over a chair, and plopped onto the couch falling against the blankets and pillow that Katie had set out for him.

Seated across from the couch, Emil greeted the house guest. "Long day."

"Feels like three days in one."

"Something to eat? To drink?"

"Yeah, maybe…"

Before Al could even state his request, Katie walked out of the kitchen carrying a plate with several sausage sandwiches and a beer. Placing the items on the coffee table between the guys, she took a seat on the arm of the chair next to her husband.

As he inhaled two sandwiches and three quarters of the beer, Al's body slowly became one with the couch. Al started a third sandwich and began to share the events of the day. "One helluva mess." Lowering the sandwich to his lap and shaking his head, Al uttered the phrase a second time. "One helluva mess." Somehow saying it a second time made it true. "Did you ever have the experience where you knew something bad had happened even before you knew what it was?"

Katie was about to describe how, when she was teenager, she knew that her grandma had passed away before her mother entered her room and shared the sad news but, the weight of Emil's hand on her thigh kept her from speaking.

"For some unexplainable reason, I decided to drive over to the jail before church. The moment the key slid into the lock I knew things on the other side of the door were not right. I felt it in my gut. I stepped into the outer office and I heard the hearts pounding within the chests of everyone in the room. All I saw was the crown of every officer. Finally, a weak voice whispered, 'Sheriff, you better come see.'"

He drained the remainder of his beer. Rather than ask for another he went into the kitchen and returned with a beer in each hand. As he stepped around the coffee table, he handed one to Emil. Emil raised a hand to signal he was good, but Al shoved the bottle at him anyway telling him that he might need it before he finished describing the scene in the cell.

The warning caused Katie to ask if she should leave. Her question was directed as much to Emil as it was to Al.

Al didn't hesitate to offer his opinion. "If you don't want the image imprinted into your memory, you probably don't want to stay."

Turning towards Emil, Katie received similar advice. With a kiss on her husband's cheek, Katie excused herself.

Al waited until Katie climbed the stairs before he continued. "Honestly, I don't think there is enough chlorine in the county."

"Are you saying…? How? How is that possible? I mean, didn't you take away any items that might…"

"Of course we did." An edge of anger was present in Al's voice. "And, that's part of the reason for the investigation. The state investigator will arrive at eleven this morning to determine what happened and if we are liable."

"So, what did happen, Al?"

"I don't know. The best I can piece together is that sometime late on Saturday night, Debra requested a different uniform, complaining that hers' was too big and continued to fall off her shoulders. The guard informed her that was not possible. Supposedly, she then started to cry and asked if she could at least have a safety pin to pull the top together."

"And with a safety pin she was able to..." Emil paused not quite sure what he wanted to say.

"Oh yeah, not only bleed out, but disfigure..." It was obvious as Al shared the details that he was no longer in this living room but back in the jail cell. The anguish carved across his face portrayed the horror he encountered. "She not only wanted to end her life, she wanted to punish her parents in the process."

For the longest time the two men sat in silence, sipping their beer and staring about the room without focusing on any one item. The realization of the mental unhealthiness that could enable a person to inflict so much pain upon her body, was more than either of them could comprehend.

Emil, with his eyes closed, shook his head before he tilted it back against the chair. He sat like this for several minutes until he wiped his entire face with his hand and then proceeded to speak as his chin dropped towards his chest. "You hinted that you might have news about Vanessa, care to share?"

From his front right shirt pocket, Al pulled a small notebook. He flipped through several pages until he located the specifics he wanted to share. "Since last Wednesday she has met the same person on three separate occasions at what I would identify as secluded locations. The first two meetings she drove in circles and back tracked for a good ten minutes, as though attempting to make sure she wasn't being followed. The third meeting, midafternoon on Saturday, Vanessa arrived first and waited twenty minutes for the other party to arrive."

"Were you able to hear the conversation between Vanessa and the other individual? Were you able to see if anything transpired between them?"

"The locations, two county parks and a field approach made it impossible to get close without being spotted."

"A field approach? Are you kidding me?"

"It was Friday night after the basketball game and the gravel road was seldom traveled."

"So clearly, based on the meeting spots, these two didn't want to be seen together in public."

"Yeah, I would say that is a very safe conclusion."

"At this point, do you have any idea why the secrecy?"

"I have a pretty good idea, but honestly, nothing at this point that would suggest a crime has been committed."

"Wait, wait, wait, a crime?" Confusion was written all across Emil's face. The conversation took a curve he didn't see coming. "Al, what are you taking ab...?" Emil sat like a piece of petrified wood until the wood was cast ashore and he could see the entire picture. "Oh my God, she's not meeting a kid. Al, who it is?"

"First, it's still an investigation and I can't tell you and second, as I just said, I don't know a crime has been..."

"Will you stop with that law enforcement crap and tell me!" If Katie had been asleep she was awake now as Emil's voice rattled the china in the china cabinet.

"Emil, I promise, you will be the first to know. I need more evidence, because honestly, a part of me can't believe this person is the father of Vanessa's baby. Yet..."

Emil completed the sentence. "Yet, as of right now, it certainly looks that way. Right?"

"Yeah."

"So, when will you have enough evidence to tell me who this is and to bring this pervert in for questioning?"

"I am tracking down a lead right now and depending on if and when they meet next, I might just show up and ask what's going on."

Emil worked to digest everything Al shared as he nursed the bottle of beer. With his mouth half full he suddenly spit a mist of the contents onto his pants and the coffee table and said, "These two aren't still...Oh, Al, tell me it's not happening."

"No, nothing happened during these three meetings."

Emil breathed a sigh of relief.

"My guess is that Vanessa is making some sort of demand of her rapist."

"Rape? Are you serious?"

"It's the only way I can make sense of this relationship, if indeed, this is the father of her baby."

"Al, you need to tell me who this is. What is she doing meeting with her rapist? I have a good relationship with Vanessa. I will be able to help her."

"Maybe so, but if this is the father and I share that name with you, and you act on it, there is a good chance the court will throw out any legal action. And if this is not the father, but a concerned citizen trying to help a wayward young woman, my job is toast. You just need to be patient."

"Patient? Like I am already, waiting for you to locate the baby Jesus?"

"Yeah, just like that my friend." Al set his empty bottle on the coffee table.

Emil knew he crossed the line and should apologize but, he was too angry. The whole thing about seventy times seven didn't seem to apply to this situation. Instead he said, "It's late, I think we both need the sleep."

Emil arose earlier than usual with the expectation that he would catch Al before he left and he could apologize to him. Unfortunately, the only evidence that suggested Al spent the night was a few grounds of coffee at the bottom of a cup. The blankets were neatly folded, and the pillow rested squarely atop the pile.

After a lengthy shower to rinse off the reminders of previous day, Emil still felt anxious about missing Al that morning and frustrated with himself for his childish behavior. He decided that the best place for breakfast would be at the cafe. He chuckled to himself as he admitted that he was curious to hear the chatter surrounding yesterday's tragic event.

He arrived shortly before seven and already the Uptown Cafe was three-quarters filled. Since more than half of the people were members of First Lutheran he spent the better part of the hour moving from table to table greeting folks, listening, and of course, drinking more coffee. The Uptown Cafe was known for its dark, strong coffee. Rumor was by eight-thirty or nine o'clock a spoon would stand upright in the cup.

The details of the events at the jail varied widely. About the only consistent fact was that with each table Emil visited the details grew more graphic and gruesome. And of course, because there was the connection to the Dempewolf's, Stanley and Thom, church members assumed that Pastor Fischer had inside information.

Respecting the office of clergy and all the responsibilities that went with such a position, Emil consistently spoke the same words. "Yes, this is a very trying time for Thom, obviously, and of course, for his parents. As well as for the Vollmer's, therefore, we need to remember them all in our prayers and ask God to provide the strength necessary to move forward."

It was about quarter past eight when Jerome Lietzau stepped into the cafe accompanied by Walter. It was Walter who first noticed Emil and pushed Jerome towards the table to join the small group in the corner booth.

"Good morning, Pastor. Jerome and I just came from the church. I was there making sure the sidewalks were clear of snow. And Jerome…" Walter paused and looked at Jerome.

"Ya,.." Jerome stopped for several seconds. "I just stopped by to make sure everything was working."

Walter jumped in, "Sure is sad news from the jail, ha?"

"It sure is, Walter. I just can't imagine what the Vollmer's are experiencing." Emil permitted himself to speak honestly to Walter.

"Have you spoken with Thom? How is he doing?"

"Thanks for asking, Jerome." At that point Emil decided he needed to offer the same response he had shared all morning. "This is a very…"

When the waitress arrived to take Jerome and Walter's orders, Jerome asked Emil if he had eaten yet and then insisted on buying the pastor breakfast. As they waited for the food to arrive, Jerome apologized for changing the topic of conversation and then proceeded to ask, "I gotta tell you, Pastor, folks are getting nervous that there is still no baby Jesus, any news?"

Emil was thankful to be able to discuss something other than the events from yesterday but at the same time he also wondered if this was Jerome's true motive for visiting the church. He had a feeling that Jerome was after something else. It felt at times like the two of them were playing a cat and mouse game. With so many other people around, Emil wasn't about to question Jerome. Instead, he stuck to the script.

"Unfortunately, no. There is nothing new. I actually asked Sheriff Schuette yesterday if there were any new leads and he said, 'It's pretty cold.'"

"Does that mean the manger will be empty this year?"

Emil hadn't thought about it in that manner, but Jerome's question made him stop and think about all the images that created. He wanted to say, yeah, considering everything that had happened, it certainly felt like the manger was empty. But, the words that drifted across the table, just as the food arrived were, "It does unless you have another solution."

Between mouth fulls of food and listening to the conversation at the table which drifted from local to global events, Emil continued to be gripped by the notion of an empty manger. Could he and would it be appropriate to preach on Sunday, the last Sunday before Christmas, about the empty manger? Was that God's Word or simply his word, his agenda?

Thanking Jerome for breakfast and leaving the Cafe first, Emil felt Jerome's eyes watching him depart and the idea of a cat and mouse game returned. There was something that Jerome was searching for, but he was unable to ask. Clearly, whatever he sought wasn't addressed at breakfast.

Emil spent the remainder of the morning at the school along with Father Neubarth and the school counselor offering comfort to students shook by the reports of Debra's passing. Many students didn't learn of the event until they stepped into the school. After lunch Emil made multiple stops, first the jail, followed by Stanley and Greta's country estates, and eventually the Vollmer's, where Father Neubarth was meeting with the family planning the funeral scheduled for Friday morning.

Emil was frustrated that he hadn't been able to connect with Al all day. He wasn't at the county jail when he stopped to see Thom and, even though he left a message for the sheriff to call, Katie reported that she hadn't heard from Al. He had to accept the fact that any apology would have to wait until Tuesday.

CHAPTER 17

Emil got to his office a few minutes before eight on Tuesday morning. He needed to stay put behind his desk and prepare sermons for the next three worship services. Especially considering the fact that sermons two and three would be delivered to a full house on Christmas Eve and Christmas morning. Plus, there were devotions to create for the council meeting that evening, to say nothing of mentally preparing for the meeting itself. Unless the baby Jesus miraculously appeared within the next twelve hours, the eight o'clock meeting could be intense, if not heated. And since that wasn't likely, that a second miracle delivery would happen, Emil was sure Jerome would make life difficult.

Surprisingly, Jerome wasn't present when the meeting started. Karl Mueller, the Vice Chair, was forced to call the meeting to order. The council members couldn't believe that Jerome would miss this meeting or that he hadn't called Pastor Fischer or Rozella to let them know he couldn't make it, Something serious had to have come up at the last minute.

Without Jerome present to drag the matter out, the council decided that if the baby Jesus was not found by Christmas Eve a doll would be wrapped and placed in the manger. Liam Mueller made a motion that if the figurine was not found, a new baby Jesus be purchased after Christmas, hoping that such an item would be on sale. The remainder of the meeting moved along smoothly and a motion to adjourn was moved and seconded and members were filing out of the church by nine-thirty.

As others departed, Walter busied himself in the library while he waited to talk to Pastor Fischer in private. "I'm concerned about Jerome."

"Yes, me too, this is unlike him."

"No, I don't just mean about tonight, about everything for the past several weeks. Jerome just hasn't been himself. He seems preoccupied…" Walter paused for a moment and then finished, "with something, but every time I ask him what's wrong he gets angry and says, 'nothing.' At first, I thought it was the figurine issue, and then the cancellation of the Kris Kringle festival, I even wondered if the Cuban Missile Crisis was affecting him. Now, I just don't know."

"Funny you should say that, Walter, because I have been thinking the same thing the past week. Jerome appears here in the church, or at my office door, and doesn't have a purpose. Sometimes he disappears as quickly as he appears, and I have no idea what's up."

Rubbing his forehead, Walter asks, "Do you think we should drive over to his house and make sure he's okay?"

"We could, but I'm afraid he might get angry that we're checking up on him. He already seems concerned that we don't trust him, or, more accurately, that I don't trust him."

Walter only agreed to go home when Pastor Fischer agreed to go to Lieztau's house if Jerome didn't show up for morning coffee on Wednesday.

Emil's thoughts were still burdened with Jerome as he

poured himself a glass of milk as a night cap before getting ready for bed. He knew Walter was right, they should have driven over to Jerome's place to check on him. To suppress the gnawing feeling Emil decided a phone call would be equally as effective. As he extended his arm to pick up the receiver and dial the number, the phone rang. The sound startled him, he dropped back two steps, striking the table behind him before he realized what happened. Recovering, he grabbed the phone on the third ring and spoke, "This is Pastor Fischer." He felt silly being so formal because he fully expected Al to be on the other end.

The noise coming through the receiver was ear piercing. First there was screaming, followed by crying and then more hysteria. Not a single word was discernable or audible. Emil didn't have a chance to shout into the receiver before the line went dead.

Immediately Emil dialed "O" and, after the second ring tone there was an answer, "This is the operator, how may I assist you?"

Frantic, Emil raced through his request. "Can you tell me from where the previous phone call was placed to this number?"

"Yes, one moment sir." The static in the line told Emil that he hadn't been disconnected. "Sir, the call originated from the Lietzau residence."

"Operator, please notify the police and send them to the Lietzau residence. The previous phone call was filled with screaming, crying, total chaos and then the line went dead." Before the operator could respond, Emil ended the call and dialed Al's house. After five rings Emil gave up and hung up the phone.

In his pajamas Emil grabbed his winter coat, pulled on his galoshes without shoes, and inhaled the crisp night air as he raced to the car. The drive across town was filled with thoughts of what horror might await him at the Leitzau house. The mind tends to envision the worst – but the pictures in Emil's mind were nothing compared to those he encountered the moment he stepped into the house.

As his car slid to a halt on the snow packed street striking the curb across from the Lietzau house, Emil noticed immediately that the Sheriff's car was parked in the driveway, but no other police vehicles were visible. Relieved that Al was already inside it never occurred to him to wonder how Al got there so quickly.

Without stopping to knock Emil pushed through the front door. The moment his body crossed the threshold the chaos, the bedlam, hung heavy in the air and pressed upon his chest making it difficult for him to breathe. At the opposite end of the living room an ankle and a bare foot protruded from behind an orange swivel rocker. When he got closer to the foot and the ankle, he recognized the pants bunched up at the knee as belonging to Jerome. Innocently he wondered why Jerome would be lying on the wood floor. Was this the result of intoxication? It would be the last time Emil was innocent about anything in the house. Reaching the rocker, he realized Jerome's idleness wasn't due to drunkenness but the result of having been shot. That explained the odor, gunpowder.

He knelt next to the body and he checked for any signs of life. With his back to the next room he became acutely aware that he was vulnerable should the shooter or shooters still be in the house. He also wondered where Al was. He thought about calling out but that would be stupid, other than opening the front door he hadn't announced his presence. He wasn't about to start now.

Remaining in a crouched position he worked his way around the body. He noticed that he was dragging Jerome's blood on the bottoms of his shoes from the pool that was forming beneath his body. Tucked behind the rocker Emil peered into the dining room searching for any evidence of another human being. Behind the rungs of the wooden dining room chairs there appeared to be another lifeless body.

Cautiously Emil pushed himself away from the floor and stood, preparing to investigate. Silently he prayed that the body was not Jerome's wife or one of his kids. Stepping away from Jerome's torso the room spun, and Emil felt as though he was moving in slow motion. Waves of nausea flooded his core as the identity of the other body registered. His mouth was open, with all his might he was attempting to push air out of his lungs, but there was no sound. The only noise in the house came from the front door as the police barged in.

With their weapons pulled they shouted at the back of the figure in the center of the room to raise his arms into the air. Studiously, Emil obeyed and then without moving asked permission to turn and face them.

"Slowly," They ordered. As Emil turned to face them they said, "Oh, Pastor Fischer, it's you. What's going on here?"

"I don't know, but the Sheriff is down, and we need an ambulance immediately."

Cradling Al's head in his lap Emil whispered over and over, "I'm sorry. I'm sorry." Emil refused to check for vitals, even at the request of the officer, and he cursed that the ambulance wasn't arriving more quickly.

A search of the house revealed that Jerome's wife and two kids were hiding in the basement behind the furnace. Wisely, the officer who found them kept the boys and their mother downstairs until the bodies were removed from the house; since there was no way to exit the house without walking past their father.

With the bodies removed and two blankets draped carefully over the pools of blood, Jerome's family was escorted out of the house and transported to their relative's house where they would spend the night. The only questioning to occur that evening was directed towards Jerome's wife and it was simple. "Do you know what happened?"

Sitting in her parent's house, with her children safely tucked in bed with their grandpa reading them a bedtime story, Lina, Jerome's wife, started to recount the events.

"I answered the door and it was Sheriff Schuette. He asked if Jerome was home and if he could speak with him. As he came into the living room he asked if I could take the boys to another room. I asked what this was about and he said, 'I am afraid I need to arrest your husband." At that point Jerome appeared and started swearing that he hadn't done anything wrong. Unfortunately, Jerome had been drinking a lot. The Sheriff asked Jerome to calm down, but he went wild. There was a lot of pushing and shoving. I'm not sure what was happening, I tried to shelter the boys. That was when I called Pastor Fischer, but before I could say anything Jerome came out of the bedroom with a gun and the Sheriff shouted for me to get the kids out of the house. The doorway was blocked so I pushed them down the steps into the basement. I heard shots and then nothing." When she was finished, Lina fell against her mother's chest and bawled uncontrollably.

The officers offered their condolences and thanked her for being able to share what she knew. As they stepped towards the door to leave she asked, sobbing between each word, "Do . . . you . . . know . . . what . . . the . . . Sheriff . . . was . . . arresting . . . my . . . husband . . . for . . . ?"

Emil followed the ambulance to the hospital and into the emergency room where he was ushered into the waiting room. The nurse gave him several towels that he could use to clean some of the blood from his body and clothing.

When the officers arrived at the hospital to check on the Sheriff and question Pastor Fischer, they found Emil slumped down in a chair in a dimly lit waiting room. One of the nurses caught the officers as they entered the hospital and informed them that Sheriff Schuette was DOA and for the Pastor's own safety they were keeping him until someone could take him home. The staff had determined that Pastor Fischer wasn't stable enough to drive himself.

"Pastor Fischer, we are sorry, we know that Sheriff Schuette..." the officer paused momentarily before concluding his condolences, "Al, wasn't only a member of the church, but he was a good friend."

"Thank you, gentlemen." Emil straightened in the chair. "Yes, he was a good friend. It's funny, usually when Al was called to intervene with a member from church, he would call me and ask me to go along, he never called this time. I think he may have had a feeling this one might blow up on him."

"We know this is a difficult time, but do you have any idea why he was at the Lietzau residence to arrest Jerome?"

Emil's eyes grew wide and his head jerked back. "Arrest Jerome?" It all made sense.

"Yes, that's what Jerome's wife said, the sheriff came to arrest Jerome. Any idea why?"

Emil didn't answer immediately. Instead, he dropped back into the chair and starred off as though attempting to recall any conversation that might offer a clue. When he did finally speak it was short and to the point. "Nope. I have no idea." The second time that evening he knowingly lied. He lied because now there was the possibility for Vanessa to move forward without having to publicly endure the humiliation of carrying Jerome's child. Just when he thought he vindicated himself for lying his internal voice spoke, what if, what if there are others? What if Debra's need to leave Germantown was because of Jerome? What if? He heard Al's voice, "This will shake the entire town."

Refusing to let the officers transport him home, Emil used the trip to figure out how he would break the news to Katie. Hopefully, he could sneak into the house and crawl into bed without waking her. That would, at least, provide a few extra hours to develop a plan.

The drive to Al's house was completed in silence. The previous hour had resulted in emotional exhaustion and neither Emil nor Katie had the strength to talk. Despite having several additional hours to devise a plan for how best to share the horrible news of Al's death, Emil simply grabbed Katie's hand as she attempted to roll out of bed and blurted out, "Al was shot last night, he didn't survive."

"That's not something to joke about, what, is he going to burst into the room and scare me?"

"I'm serious Katie. Al went to Jerome's house last night to arrest him and there was a gunfight, and both were killed."

"Jerome? Arrested? Our Jerome?" The down feathers in the pillow fluffed from one side to the other as Katie's head shook in disbelief. "Why would Al want to arrest Jerome?" And she paused. "Oh my god, Al didn't think Jerome stole the figurine?"

"No, it wasn't anything like that. It doesn't really matter what the reason was, both are dead."

"What do you mean it doesn't matter, of course it matters."

"No, it doesn't. It won't bring them back so just drop it."

"Emil, what's this abo…" Katie raised up on her elbow and stared directly at her husband. "You, you weren't there were you? I mean, were you in danger? I knew it would come to . . ."

Emil stopped her before she worked herself into a frenzy. "No, Katie, unfortunately I arrived afterwards."

"Unfortunately? What do you mean, unfortunately? You're not stupid enough to think you could have prevented this, are you?"

"You never know, you just never know."

"Of course I know. If you had been there you might have been shot too."

"But, I wasn't there, and I wasn't shot, so stop it. Jerome and Al are dead."

"Yes," she dropped back to the bed, "I'm sorry. I just worry about you."

She rolled against her husband to comfort him as he mourned the loss of two friends. She no longer tried to speak; she understood words didn't exist to fill the emptiness Emil was feeling. She understood because her face too was washed by her own tears and the hole in the pit of her stomach was expanding as she thought about life without Al.

Before climbing the stairwell the previous evening, Emil had removed the blankets and pillow Katie set out for Al in case he arrived to spend the night. Breakfast was a forced ordeal as the conversation focused on the reality that Al didn't have any family and that it was probably up to them to collect clothes to deliver to the funeral director, it was up to them to lock down Al's house, it was up to them to plan Al's funeral. A funeral, Emil decided would happen on Christmas Eve no matter what objections might be cast.

The drive to Al's house was completed in silence as the two of them planned how to complete their assignments as quickly and as efficiently as possible. Neither of them was mentally ready to spend a lengthy duration in their friend's house. They quickly located the key buried beneath the snow and under the pot that was filled with geraniums every summer and entered the house. It smelled of stale bacon. Katie went directly into the kitchen to empty the refrigerator and Emil went upstairs to the bedroom to fetch Al's suit. He knew some people in the community would suggest Al should be buried in his uniform and others would demand a military funeral, but these people didn't know Al. Al wanted nothing to do with pomp and circumstance, keep it simple was Al's mantra.

On his return to the kitchen, Emil checked the thermostat and set it at 50 degrees and then proceeded to check that every window was locked, and the back door was secure.

Leaving the house, Katie questioned why Emil didn't return the key to its hiding place. His response was both honest and sarcastic, "What for? It's not like Al needs the key anymore. Who else besides you or I need to be in the house?" With his hand in his pants pocket he deposited the key and as they walked back to the car the weight of the metal pushed the key downward until he felt it rubbing against his thigh.

He wouldn't reach for the key again until Friday evening.

CHAPTER 18

Germantown, as well as the entire county, was in an uproar questioning what was more threating to the safety and security of the people, the Russians or their neighbors? It was less than a week until Christmas, but it certainly didn't feel like it nor did it always look like it. Within less than a week, the death of three individuals, spanning three generations, caused people to oil locks that had rusted tight, caused people to keep their children home from school, caused people to question elected leaders, and caused some people to fold their hands and other people to shake their fist all at the same God.

What unnerved Emil was that the people did not know the story behind Jerome's death or for that matter, Sheriff Schuette's. He categorically feared that if the truth ever became known the people would not be set free but would become enslaved to fear and panic. Emil himself wasn't fully aware of the evidence Al had collected against Jerome but he hoped by rummaging through Al's belongings he would find all the missing pieces. Al, on several occasions, had shared that he kept many of the critical pieces of an investigation at home because he didn't trust all his employees. The one thing Emil vowed was that he would not perform any inspection until after Jerome's funeral on Saturday.

Multiple gasps were heard Friday morning when Thom entered the sanctuary and took a seat next to his parents. The gasps turned to mumbles as everyone attempted to determine how he was permitted to be present at such a sacred event? Truth was, Thom had been brought to the funeral by the acting Sheriff. The interim Sheriff, who had been born and raised on the opposite end of the county, entertained Emil's request to permit Thom to attend Debra's funeral service. It was agreed that immediately following the burial, Thom would be transported back to jail.

Attending Debra's funeral with Katie, Emil prayed that there was not a connection between Debra and Jerome. He prayed that the community would not punish the Vollmer family for what was an apparent suicide. He also thanked God that Father Neubarth was willing to set aside the Papal rule and conduct the funeral in the church and for the burial to be within the Catholic cemetery. It was a huge risk if the Bishop found out but for an aging priest, the risk seemed minimal. Father Neubarth's commentary on the risk was tongue in cheek for Emil, "What's the worst that could happen, I spend an extra year or two in Purgatory."

For Emil, Debra's funeral blended into the events surrounding Jerome's funeral the next day. Other than the presence of extended family from out of town, the same town's people attended both funerals and the theme at the Catholic Church and First Lutheran Church was basically the same. During the holiday season, such untimely deaths, such tragic events contradict the joy that is supposed to fill every heart and yet, that is precisely why both communities gather to celebrate Christmas.

The greater stress for Emil occurred last Wednesday afternoon when Vanessa stood in the doorway of the church office. This time rather than ask which chair to take she lowered herself onto the wooden chair. The rotation of her hand on her stomach never stopped. When Emil quietly said, "Jerome is the father," she nodded.

Like the burst of a dam a flood of questions raced to the back of Emil's lips, but only one, only one question was presented to Vanessa and it wasn't stated as a question, as much as a directive, "Tell me how this happened."

The hand movement ceased, she looked directly at him and said, "What difference does it make now? He's dead, no one ever needs to know. My parents think it's David's and I want this child to be David's."

Emil objected as pastorally as possible, "But, Vanessa, there is more here than a child."

"Oh really!" She shouted.

It was the first time Emil could ever recall Vanessa displaying any anger.

She continued, "And who is carrying this child? I'm sorry Pastor but you don't have any idea what this is about, and I suggest, for everyone's safety, you let things be."

"And if I can't?

"You can, you're just electing not to. I am asking, I am begging you, just stop. I can live with this and my child can live with this."

Emil sat back. He marveled at how this sixteen-year-old girl had become an adult woman nearly over night. She was making decisions for herself and her unborn child. What

155

bothered him was, were these wise decisions? Something was scaring her into demanding that he remain silent. This fear would obviously keep her from providing greater clarity.

Slowly he brought his body back toward the edge of the desk, with his hands folded upon the desk top he spoke, "Vanessa, for the time being, I will stop pressing you for answers, but I can't promise you that I will keep quiet. Two people are dead, the father of your child and my best friend," hearing himself acknowledge Al as his best friend nearly took his breath away, "and who knows possibly how many more."

Vanessa rose from the chair, pulled on her coat and shook her head as she walked towards the door. At the door she stopped and turned back and delivered her final comment. "I wish I could tell you, I really do, but if you knew the truth, your life could be in danger."

With the final Advent sermon prepared, Emil was free to leave his office late Saturday afternoon as the last of Jerome's extended family departed. Such freedom resulted in him making his way to Al's house.

The walk from the driveway to the front porch was cold as the wind swirled down the hillside and across the river and slammed against the house. He reached deep into his pants pocket to find the key to unlock the front door and enable him to search the house from top to bottom. The task was to find evidence linked to Jerome; in the days and weeks that followed the task would be to empty the house, to clean it, and to place it on the market. His gloves and scarf dropped just beyond the swing of the door and his coat four steps further into the house as he went directly to the roll top desk that stood in the living room positioned squarely between two windows.

His efforts were rewarded immediately. The first cubby he investigated was stuffed with 3 x 4 inch slips of papers scribbled with notes, several pictures, and four sheets of paper that were copies of medical bills originating three counties away. Medical was a polite way, even a sanitary way of referring to the services offered. "Medical" was the word Al scrolled across the top of each page, that was the verbiage Emil would use knowing it was something entirely different. Everything Emil hoped would not be revealed stared him in the face. Jerome wasn't only using young women for his own pleasure he was making them available to other men. The missing piece was, why? Why would these young women allow themselves to be used in such manner? What did Jerome have on them to force them to give up all self-respect? Vanessa and Debra were only two of a handful of names. Based on the identity of the young women this wasn't limited to Germantown. The evils of Jerome's work stretched well beyond the valley.

Engrossed in the evidence staring him in the face, Emil never heard the front door open, nor did he realize that he was no longer alone in the living room. To gain Emil's attention the person cleared his throat. Emil jumped, dropping the contents from his hands as he prepared to brace his fall into the desk.

Sitting half on the desk and supporting the reminder of his weight with the free hand that was not holding his chest, Emil's response was disrupted by deep breaths. "Walter . . . don't . . . do . . . that . . ." Picking up the scraps of paper that fell to the floor, Emil continued. "How did you get in here?"

Kneeling beside Emil to assist in the collection of items, Walter answered. "I saw your car in the driveway and the door wasn't locked. I figured you might need some help."

Standing and placing the items on the desk top Emil thanked Walter and, almost as an afterthought he added, "Why would you think I might need help?"

"You're trying to find an explanation to the Sheriff's death, aren't you?"

Emil couldn't believe what he was hearing. This wasn't the Walter he had come to know. The person standing next to him spoke with clarity and with a tenor he would never associate with Walter. He heard himself answering before he processed the answer. "Yeah, I guess I am."

Looking very closely at Walter, Emil saw something he never noticed before. It partially angered him as he prided himself on being able to "read" people and it also intrigued him. Sizing up the man who stood before him, as someone who possessed knowledge, insight, and possibly even wisdom, Walter no longer played the part of a naïve, even bumbling failure. Walter took on the characteristics of his name, Ruler of the Army. Words surfaced from Emil's lips before he could analyze what he said. "You know, don't you?" The words were framed as a question, but Emil meant it as a rhetorical question.

Stepping back from the edge of the roll top desk Walter scanned the room to locate the easy chair he sat in the last time he visited Sheriff Schuette. Seated with his legs crossed and arms resting on the arms of the chair, Walter nodded as he spoke, "Yes. I know."

Emil slid further back on the desk and inquired, "Do others know?" Without granting Walter permission to answer, Emil processed his thought out loud. "My God, Walter, are there other men in town who…" Emil stopped himself. The very thought made him sick to his stomach. He took several deep breaths and finished his question. "Who have used these young women?" He couldn't force himself to say girls, although that's who they were.

Calmly, Walter responded, "Not as far as I know, but…"

"But?"

"That doesn't mean some of the people might not be aware of what was happening?"

"Did the Sheriff know you knew?"

"Yeah, he figured it out and he…'

"Walter, I have to stop you and ask…"

"No, I'm not. I am not part of this. And yes, you needed to ask. The Sheriff asked the same question once it was established that I knew something was happening."

"So, how, did…"

"How did I figure it out? Free time. I had the time to watch. You see, Pastor, it's not only what you see, but also, what you don't see that's important. We busy ourselves with what we see, but it might be more beneficial to busy yourself with what we don't see."

Shaking his head Emil confessed he didn't understand. "What was it you didn't see?"

The head movement stopped abruptly as Emil realized he understood, at least partially. What he didn't see previously was the connection between Walter and Sarah. Sarah's suspicion that Vanessa was pregnant originated with Walter. Things started to fall into place. Even more significant,

Sarah's awareness of happenings in the community were connected to her husband's ability to see what was there and what was not.

Walter took time to construct his response. "Before sharing what I didn't see, I need to clarify, it's also about being in the right place. And, honestly, sometimes, being in the right place is pure luck."

That wasn't what Emil wanted to hear. "Luck? Seriously?"

"The thing with Jerome started a year ago. I started going to have breakfast on Saturday mornings, which soon evolved into six days a week. We couldn't afford it, in fact, it was the last thing I should have been doing, but I needed to get out of the house and away from the farm. Jerome was also there every morning and it wasn't long before he invited me to join him and other businessmen who rolled dice, ate breakfast, and chatted about Germantown. Fortunately, I am good at dice, so I won enough to cover my breakfast most days. Even though Jerome and I, in any other context, would never have spent time together, we discovered that we had something in common, life. We never actually named it, or identified it, but it was there. I realized, and I think he did the same about me, that his life was anything but enjoyable. What I couldn't understand about him was why?? So, with time on my hands I decided to take a look."

"You followed him?"

"I followed him, I watched him, I couldn't figure out how the life of an insurance salesman could be anything but good."

"And what did you see? Or, should I say, what didn't you see?"

"I didn't see failure. Obviously, I didn't know if every visit resulted in a policy, a renewal, or an increase, but if even half were anything, he was financially in good shape. Unless . . ."

Walter's long pause forced Emil to speak, "Unless what?"

"Unless...well...unless some of these house calls had nothing to do with insurance." Once I started to pay attention I noticed that once a week he was visiting the same homes. And then I discovered that he was meeting clients not only in their homes but at various places in the community."

"Clients?"

"Yeah, that's what Jerome called them."

"He told you he was meeting with these young women and referred to them as clients?"

"Heavens no. He told me on several occasions his agenda for the day which included meeting with several clients and when I followed him he was meeting with the girls."

"Any idea what hold he had on them that enabled him to control them?"

"Money."

"That's all it was, money?"

"Well, it was more complicated than that, but it all came down to money. As a smooth-talking salesman, once Jerome had done the surveillance work of determining who was an easy mark, it didn't take much to convince these girls that he could give them a future they could only dream about. He targeted girls whose families were struggling financially, or girls who lacked confidence, self-esteem, girls who needed a father figure who would complement them and pay them attention. Of course, once they realized what the future actually held it was too late."

"Why didn't they come forward?"

"Think about it, Pastor, who is going to believe the word of a sixteen-year-old over a forty something church-going businessman? He had them convinced that no one would ever believe them. Did Vanessa ever reveal what was going on?"

"No." Sadly, Emil had to acknowledge the truth as painful as it was.

"You are viewing them as a group, but they were never a group. I don't think any of the girls knew that she wasn't the only one. Jerome was very careful about keeping them apart."

Emil again found himself wondering who the person seated before him was. Walter had never revealed himself in this manner. There was an air of confidence and authority. It was as though the roles completely switched between the two of them. Emil was seeking answers from Walter. "What was in it for Jerome? What am I not seeing?"

Walter laughed, he couldn't help himself.

Interpreting the laugh as a faux pas on his part Emil attempt to clarify his question. "You know what I mean. I mean beyond the physical and the money, or was that it?"

Walter pulled the cigarette wraps from his shirt pocket and American Spirit tobacco from the back pocket of his pants. Packing the shredded strains of tobacco onto the paper wrap, he rolled the single sheet and carefully ran his tongue along the edge to seal his cigarette. After he inhaled the nicotine deep into his body he sunk deeper into the chair as he invited Emil to journey back in time. "To understand who Jerome had become you need to go back to his childhood. As someone new to Germantown there would be no reason you would know this, but it is important."

"New to Germantown" the words hung in the air in Al's living room taunting Emil with the fact that he was an outsider. As the word invaded his body he recalled the conversation with an elderly shut-in, eighty-eight years young, who was widowed for the last forty years of her life. She married a young man from Germantown and together they raised three children, each went on to have successful careers. After twenty-eight years of marriage her husband unexpectedly passed away. She elected to stay in the community which she considered her home. Yet, tearfully, she explained that after living in Germantown for sixty-eight years she was still identified as an outsider. Emil had to accept the fact that, no matter the number of years he lived in Germantown, he would always be an outsider, someone "new to Germantown."

Walter, unaware that Emil had drifted into an experience from the past, continued to describe Jerome's early years. "He was a mamma's boy. His father, while he was still in the picture, never hid his disappointment with his son. In an effort to make Jerome into a man he humiliated his son. He did this in front of Jerome's friends and it didn't take long for them to pick up on the names. Jerome became known as Lietz the Tits, and worse. It didn't help that he was overweight and uncoordinated. Even the gym teacher saw Jerome as an easy target. To motivate the middle schoolers', he called out Jerome. "With a little effort and focus everyone can learn how to chew gum and walk, even Mr. Lietzau."

Shaking his head in total disbelief Emil could only offer, "Amazing what we would tolerate, back in the day, in the name of developing character."

Ignoring Emil's comment, Walter continued. "In high school little changed. Jerome continued to be the kid on the outside looking to become a part of the in group. It just never happened. I don't remember exactly when Jerome's dad left, it might have been between eighth and ninth grade, but even his departure, which Jerome welcomed momentarily, was laced with humiliation for Jerome. His dad moved three counties over where he set up a home with a former prostitute and her three children. Far as I know, Jerome never saw his father again, yet he was identified as his father's son. And that added to his humiliation."

"That certainly doesn't sound fair." Emil had become completely engulfed in the story. He saw Jerome as a victim and felt sorry for him.

"Fair? Come on Pastor. You remember high school, what was fair?"

Naively, Emil had hoped that society had progressed beyond such childish behavior. Truth was, it wasn't limited to childhood, such behavior continued long into adulthood for many folks.

"After high school he jumped from job to job. It was like he was always trying to impress others and the harder he tried the more he failed. Some of the jobs he quit and others he was fired from. Things were bad; he was living at home, no friends to speak of, no girls willing to be seen with him, until he…" Walter shrugged as he described the fortunate turn of events, "just sort of fell into an insurance job. Old man Ritter," he paused for a moment as he thought, "funny, I don't think I ever did know his first name, put the word out that he was searching for someone to join the business. He was getting along in years and no longer able to keep up with the demands of the jobs. The qualifications he put out for the position were quite simple: someone who didn't mind working long hours, someone who was self-motivated, and most important of all, someone who could talk to anyone. The moment Jerome learned of the opening, he knew that was the job for him. And he was right."

Walter stopped describing the life events of Jerome and looked towards the kitchen. "You don't suppose there are any beers still in the fridge, do you?"

Smiling, Emil said, "I left the beer when we cleaned out the refrigerator of perishables."

With both men seated and holding a cold beer, Walter picked up where he left off. "Slowly Jerome's image in the community changed. He met a young woman, a few years younger, from town, he moved into the apartment above the insurance office, and he was selling insurance policies. It wasn't long before he and Lina were married and moved out of the apartment and into their house. Old man Ritter was so impressed with Jerome that when he decided to retire he offered Jerome the opportunity to buy the business. With the assistance of a friendly banker, Jerome was able to secure a loan."

Emil interrupted Walter when he took a sip of his beer. "Up until the last part of this story it sounded like it was going to be the classic case of scared victim seeking to compensate for his terrible childhood. It was about the power he could possess, about being in control, about being important and being flattered that cute teenage girls were needing him. The physical gratification was certainly present but, it really was about so much more. But, now, I'm not so sure. Jerome apparently had been able to move . . ."

Walter waved his hand to stop his pastor. "Jerome never did move beyond the pain of his childhood."

"What makes you think that?"

"Because it came up many times."

"You mean, he talked about his childhood?"

Walter shrugged and took his time as he answered. "Not right way but once he started, it all became clear. There was anger, lots of anger, and directed towards half the people in Germantown."

"So, it was all about power, and control?"

"It was about impressing others, proving he wasn't the labels placed on him but, it was never enough. It was never enough for him to silence the voices in his head."

"He heard voices?" Emil's brow wrinkled creating deep farrows across his forehead. "He told you that?"

"It happened by accident one morning in the café. Karl Mueller stopped by the table to say hi. It was social, all very friendly, but after Karl walked away, Jerome was different."

"Different, how?"

"Before I could swallow a mouth full of coffee he went from being an extrovert to being withdrawn. He rubbed his temples and kept his head down. He looked terrible. He looked sick. I offered to drive him home and once in the car he opened up. He described how when he meets people who once teased him, he could still hear the words from his childhood." Emil set his empty bottle next to his chair and moved Jerome's story to its sad conclusion. "What brought the case out into the open? Did you go to the Sheriff?"

"Nope." Walter chuckled in a very sarcastic manner before he continued. "You'll never guess where the break in the case originated."

"You're right, I have no idea.

"It came from the jail."

"The jail?" The crease in Emil's forehead was even deeper now.

"Get this. It was Debra."

"She was a part of this sadistic activity, my god, what she must have gone through to have reached a point where she hated life." Emil had to stop to keep the tears from dropping from the corner of eyes. He wished there was beer left in the bottle so that he might disguise the reason for his silence. Little did he know, Walter had been there many times, many times. Confident he could speak without his voice quivering he continued, "What, Debra told what had happened to her?"

"No, it all came together with a single phone call."

"A phone call? From, Debra?"

"Guess who she called?

"Noooo." Realizing the truth, Emil, beneath the pressure of the moment couldn't stop the force of air that left his body like a balloon escaping the fingers of a child.

Nodding, Walter confirmed the truth; Debra called Jerome because she trusted him more than her parents. That single phone call put the Sheriff on the track of Jerome.

"I can't imagine that the Sheriff was aware of your knowledge concerning Jerome's actions. How did the two of you connect?"

"It happened…" Walter stopped and smiled. "That part of the story requires another one of the Sheriff's beers."

After a quick visit to the bathroom Walter described how the Sheriff knocked on the window of his car.

Emil looked bewildered but didn't interrupt Walter.

"When I was following Jerome, I noticed that another car was also following Jerome. It was the Sheriff's. Since I knew Jerome's routine and the various locations he would meet the girls, once I saw the Sheriff was tailing Jerome I increased my distance. Sometimes my tailing was nothing more than a drive by to confirm that Jerome stopped at one of the locations and other times to catch a glimpse of the girl, I would park the car as far away as possible and use binoculars."

Emil nodded intently.

"It was the third day after noticing that the Sheriff was also following Jerome when he appeared at the side of my car. I thought I had been careful not to call attention to myself so when Jerome pulled into county park number three, I entered the park, a good ten minutes later, and drove to the south end. I was pretty sure Jerome's vehicle would be parked on the north end below the hill beside a huge snow pile to conceal its presence. From my location it was impossible to see Jerome's car or the person he was meeting. I would have to walk along the lake shore and climb the hill to peer down on the rendezvous. I had just turned the collar of my coat up and pulled my scarf tighter to block the wind from my neck when knuckles wrapped against the glass. I nearly peed in my pants."

Emil couldn't help but laugh at the thought of Walter peeing on himself. Laughing at Walter's expense he managed to ask, "It was the Sheriff?"

"Yeah, but for a split second I thought it might be Jerome

and my mind raced to explain why I was at the county park, as it was, I had to explain."

Still finding humor in Walter's predicament, Emil added, "Who would have ever thought having a Sheriff knock on your car window would be a good thing?"

Walter ignored that comment and continued. "I don't know where he came from. He wasn't following Jerome and I'm pretty sure he wasn't following me."

"Could he have been in the park before the two of you even arrived?"

"I considered that, but if he was, it had to be an accident. There would have been no way for the Sheriff to know that this was a meeting place since the two previous days Jerome met the girls at a different location."

"Is it possible that one of the girls told the Sheriff about the location?"

"I suppose, but . . ." Walter paused a good thirty seconds before finishing his response. "I seriously doubt this young woman would have told the Sheriff anything."

"Whom did he meet?"

"Vanessa." Walter whispered the name as though embarrassed to speak it aloud.

Both men sat silently contemplating what might have been the focus of such a meeting. Based on the medical receipts found in the desk Emil knew that girls in Vanessa's condition were taken to a facility several counties over to have an abortion. Walter was also aware of this "treatment" plan having followed Jerome and two different girls to the facility.

It was Emil who broke the silence. "So, after the Sheriff helped you empty your bladder, what happened?"

"That's real funny, Pastor. I said I *nearly* peed in my pants." Walter straightened up in the chair before continuing. "After getting my attention, he pointed to the other door and when I nodded, he walked around the car and slid into the front seat.

In his usual calm manner, he greeted me and then asked, "Walter, what are you doing out here?"

I thought about lying, but concluded that he knew why I was in the park. It didn't take long to share everything I knew. Together we walked the shoreline and climbed the hill just in time to witness Vanessa leaving Jerome's car and running back to her car."

"What happened then?"

"We waited until both cars spun away from the snow pile and left the park. We walked back to my car where the Sheriff told me that everything I knew was, for the time being, to be kept between the two of us and that I should stop following Jerome - that was his job."

"And you followed that directive?"

"Yes, otherwise I would have been sitting outside Jerome's house the other night when things went bad." Walter stared at the ceiling for a time before he spoke. "It's sad you know, when it really mattered, I wasn't in the right place."

Emil wasn't sure how to respond initially. He certainly hoped Walter didn't blame himself for what happened in Jerome's house but if he did, a few quickly chosen words weren't about to change his belief. There was also that notion, again, of being in the right place and it made him uncomfortable, because he didn't know what that meant. When he finally figured out what he wanted to say he was looking at the back of Walter as he was reaching for the front door.

"You leaving?"

"Yeah, it's getting late. It's been a long day and you need to go home, Pastor."

Walter was right, it had been a long day and Katie was waiting for him to get home to assist with decorating the Christmas tree. "You're right, Walter, it has been a long day and I should be getting home. Thank you for helping me see what I hadn't seen."

Walter was more than halfway through the doorway when he stopped and stepped back inside the Sheriff's house. Striking a match to light another rolled cigarette before walking to his car he addressed Emil one final time. "Pastor, I wouldn't worry about the figurine. I have a feeling the baby Jesus will be returned on Christmas Eve. And before you ask, no, I didn't take it, nor did I see who did. But, I'm pretty sure I know who did take it based on what I don't see."

CHAPTER 19

The moment Emil stepped out of the car he heard it, Christmas music. He was late, exceptionally late and even worse, he had promised. She was going to be upset with him, again.

One of the traditions Emil was adamant about was when to decorate for Christmas, which also included, when to start playing Christmas music. Everyone knew, or they should know, Advent was Advent, a time of preparation, not a time to be celebrating Christmas. How do you prepare for something if you are already overwhelmed with the celebration? Memories from Emil's childhood strengthened his strict stance on this matter. The Christmas tree in Emil's childhood house never appeared until December 23rd. The entire family would gather in the living room to trim the tree and sing Christmas songs. What Emil never realized as a young child was that date selected had nothing to do with maintaining the sanctity of Advent but was entirely for practical reasons. The placement of the tree was less than five feet from the oil burner which dried the tree out so it never lasted more than five days. But even more significant was the fact that merchants cut the price of trees in half two days before Christmas in order to clear out the lot. Emil's parents couldn't afford the luxury of a Christmas tree at full price. Learning the practical reasons as a college student didn't alter the fact that Emil was determined to postpone decorating for Christmas as long as possible.

The lyrics slapped him across the face as he pushed through the front door. "I'll have a Blue Christmas without you. I'll be so blue just thinking about you." Coming from the voice of Elvis, the words carried greater weight. He hoped it wasn't intentional, but . . . he stopped himself from drawing a formal conclusion before he spoke with Katie. Still, he was thankful that before leaving the house earlier in the day he had placed the tree he purchased at Vollmer's Grocery store in the tree stand.

Emil stepped into the living room and Katie greeted her husband, "Let me guess, the phone rang at the church as you were on your way out, you returned to answered it and you were needed to divert some crisis."

She stood in front of the tree looking so beautiful. The butter yellow mohair sweater and black pleated skirt accentuated her figure. The bob in her hair drooped ever so slightly giving her a sexy look. Elvis was now singing, "I'll be Home for Christmas," and Emil wanted to embrace her and apologize for once again leaving her alone, but instead he described the events of the afternoon.

Katie appeared uninterested in the majority of the details until Emil shared that the entire conversation with Walter took place at Al's house. At that point she took a step closer to him and interrupted him, "You went back to Al's?"

"Yes, I had a feeling that Al had evidence pertaining to Jerome at the house and so . . . ."

Again, she cut him off. "You locked it when you left, didn't you? I mean, we don't want people going through the house until we've emptied the house out all of Al's belongings."

"I did, and I have the key safely tucked away." He patted his pants pocket.

"Well, good." Softening her words, she finished. "You know how kids can be and with Al having been the Sheriff and all."

"Yes, I know your concern. We need to be careful."

Sensing that Katie had moved past her anger and would be able to enjoy what was left of the evening, Emil suggested they retire to the couch and watch TV. At the conclusion of the Gunsmoke episode Katie kissed Emil and told him to not stay up too late.

Under the glow of the lights from the Christmas tree, Emil thought about everything Walter shared. Again, he found himself wondering how it was possible that Walter lost the farm. Maybe there was more to the story of Walter and Sarah than he previously considered. The question that surfaced repeatedly was, what had he missed? Not only what had he missed related to Walter and Sarah, but related to everyone else?

Emil had prided himself in being able to be in tune with people, he could read them, or so he told himself, but... Staring at the tree Emil noticed that the tinsel distorted the light in such a manner that it cast an artificial glow. The tree appeared to be lit by more bulbs than it was.

Emil realized, at that moment, that this was not only deception, but intentional deception. Viewing his reflection in the picture window mingled with the tree he asked himself, was the same true about the people of Germantown? Was intentional deception the sin that blanketed the valley like a thick fog?

Standing next to the tree about to reach down and unplug the extension cord from the outlet he noticed the small ornament Katie had placed atop a Christmas gift last year to add flare and uniqueness to the package. The ornament was a tiny manger and baby made from olivewood. Emil reached for the ornament and held it firmly within the palm of his hand. He had forgotten Walter's prediction that the figurine would be returned. Opening his hand slightly while cradling the manger carefully he pondered, what else didn't he see?

The Sunday School Christmas Program packed the church. When Emil first arrived at First Lutheran, the Children's Christmas Program was Christmas Eve at 8:00 p.m. By the time the service ended, half the young kids were asleep and the other half was screaming in hopes of not falling asleep. His suggestion to move the program to the fourth Sunday in Advent was not well received but, with the support of Sunday School teachers who were stressed attempting to control the kids, the majority of the members looked favorably upon the decision. Plus, the fourth Sunday in Advent just meant that Christmas arrived a little earlier.

The Sunday service was transformed into a traditional Christmas program. Children performed the various roles of the nativity story starting with an Angel coming to visit Joseph, followed by Mary's visitation and the singing of the Magnificat by the entire congregation. The story unfolded as each class, starting with preschoolers, marched to the front of the church and stood proudly before mom and dad, grandma and grandpa, and sang a few carefully selected Christmas hymns followed by three or four individuals who recited a biblical passage. Unfortunately, other than mom, who knew the passage better than the child, no one could hear the children and therefore, no one knew what was being said. In the end, it didn't matter, everyone smiled and after the service each child would be told they did a great job. As the children were reunited with their families, every child received a brown paper bag filled with goodies. In addition to the religious trinkets, a cross, a bookmark with Psalm 23, and a pencil inscribed with, "Jesus Loves Me," there was an orange, an apple, a healthy handful of peanuts, several pieces of chocolate candy, and a Tootsie Pop.

Emil felt a twinge of guilt, even worse yet, panic, watching parishioners leave filled with excitement, being reinvigorated, renewed, and there was never a moment when his voice was heard. There was no sermon! Humbly he had to confess that God's message of grace will be delivered as God determines fit. Luther was correct when he said, "Next to the Word of God, music deserves the highest praise." That was the gift of the Christmas program, music. Still...

Among the last to leave the church was Liam Mueller. He busied himself with minimal tasks to appear to have a purpose, but the truth was he simply wanted to talk to Emil. When he finally arrived at the door to shake Emil's hand, it became evident why he was the last to leave. "Pastor Fischer, are you busy later this afternoon? I think it would be important for us to discuss a few things."

"I have a few things I need to take care of today, but they are all things I plan to do here at the church. What time were you thinking?"

"It really doesn't matter. Maybe, three? Would that be okay?"

"Sure. What is it you want to discuss?"

With his head turning from side to side to ensure they were alone he lowered his voice and whispered, "I really don't want to say other than it involves, Mr. Lietzau."

Nodding once, Emil assured Liam that was acceptable.

Following a quiet lunch with Katie and a thirty-minute nap, Emil informed Katie that he needed to return to church to finish Al's funeral sermon and write the Christmas Eve sermon. He also shared that Liam requested a visit later in the afternoon.

With Al's funeral message completed and set aside, and the Christmas Eve message nearly writing itself with the emphasis on "Being in the Right Place," Emil completely lost track of time. The noise of the typewriter covered Liam's entrance into the church and the climb up the stairs. It wasn't until he stood in the doorway that Emil noticed his three o'clock appointment had arrived.

"Hi Liam. Come on in and have a seat." With a wave of his hand, Emil directed his visitor to the chair directly across from him. "Give me just a minute, I need to finish one thought here or I will forget."

Holding his hand up as he took a seat, Liam assured Emil it was quite alright. "Oh, you go ahead and finish, Pastor. I'm early. Sorry about that."

Having finished typing, Emil moved the typewriter off to the side, so it wouldn't block the path between the two gentlemen. "No need to apologize. I needed a break anyway. Been working since one thirty."

Sensing Liam's nervousness, Emil decided to forgo the

small talk and get right to the issue. "You said you wanted to discuss something concerning Jerome?"

"Yes, that's right." Liam looked down at his overshoes wet with the remains of melted snow. "I…, I'm…, not sure where or what exactly to say."

"Just take your time and tell me whatever you want."

"I really don't know where to start."

"Is there a beginning? Start there."

"A beginning?"

"Since this is about Jerome, I assume there was a point where you became aware of something or gained some knowledge that you now consider important and want to share."

Liam thought for moment. "Yes, yes, Pastor, that is exactly what happened."

"Okay, start at the beginning."

Liam slid back in the chair as though he was being transported to the beginning. Slowly he started. "I remember the day, it was July sixth. I remember the day because I had just finished reading William Falkner's book, *The Reivers*. And get this, it was the very day that Falkner died. It was a Friday and I stopped at the bar for a cold one before heading home."

Emil nodded as he listened to Liam.

"I'm sitt'n at the bar, solving all the world problems with Ludwig, who has been tending bar since my dad first stepped foot in the bar at the age of twelve, when Jerome took a seat on the stool next to me. We greeted each other politely, he ordered a beer and another for me. He joined in the conversation with Ludwig, until the old guy shuffled down to the other end of the bar. At that point, Jerome brings up a new topic." Liam paused for moment as though he was still in the bar taking a sip of his beer. "Pastor, are you familiar with the plot of *The Reivers*?"

"I can't say that I am."

"Have you even heard of the book?"

"I must confess, no."

"The book is basically about three boys, not yet teenagers, who steal a car. The boys live in Mississippi and drive to Memphis where they end up at Miss Reba's."

"Miss Reba's?" Emil is totally confused.

"Yeah. Miss Reba's is . . . is . . . well, Pastor, it's a place where men go to be entertained by women."

"A brothel."

"Yep."

"Sounds like an . . . engaging read. But what does this have to do with Jerome and the bar?"

Nodding, Liam was trying to assist Emil in making the connection. "That's what Jerome started talking about."

"A brothel?"

"Not a brothel, I mean, he never mentioned a place, but instead, men being entertained by women . . ." Liam took a depth breath and clarified. "Girls, men being entertained by girls."

"Girls? I'm not following." Emil knew precisely what Liam was describing but he wanted Liam to be specific."

"Jerome was telling me about men being entertained by girls. He hinted that I could enjoy such entertainment."

"And?"

"Oh, no. Pastor, I'd never."

Raising his left hand and patting the air, Emil assured Liam he understood. "I know, Liam, I know. Did Jerome ever describe what this entertainment all included and how you could participate?"

"I think, and I can only say, I think, because he was careful to never fully state it, I think he was offering me a girl to have sex with."

"You told him no?"

"I never told him anything. I just nodded and followed along. Eventually he said, "You know where to find me if you need a little excitement in your life.""

"Did you ever tell anyone else?"

"No, but I think . . ." Again, Liam paused measuring the necessity to be honest. "Karl." With his head down, Liam attempted to be honest. "I am pretty sure that Karl was aware of what Jerome was doing with the girls."

"You mean, he met with the girls?"

"I don't know that, Pastor, I just have the feeling that he was aware of what Jerome was offering."

Emil's follow up question had more to do with the position that Karl now held in the church, council president, than it had to do with morbid curiosity. "What made you conclude he knew about the girls?"

"When I asked Karl if he was aware of anything strange about Jerome, he said, "Strange? Jerome is always strange.""

"In other words, he avoided your question."

"Exactly. And even though he would still tease Jerome, it was less aggressive than usual. Plus, and I know this for a fact, things aren't going so well at home for Karl."

"That doesn't mean…"

"I know, Pastor, but I also know my brother. I love him, but I am realistic when it comes to Karl."

"So, last month when Karl was confronting Jerome, that was for show?"

"I think it was. I happened to stop at the bar one night during the week and there was Karl and Jerome together at the bar, as though they were friends." Shaking his head, Liam continued. "That's not Karl."

Emil was silent for several minutes trying to determine how to proceed. Finally, when he spoke he brought the conversation back to the beginning. "Liam, why are you sharing this with me? Why didn't you say something sooner?"

Staring directly at Emil he answered the last question first. "You're too new here to understand, things don't work that way here, Pastor. But," he paused for a split second, "if it's all true, now that Jerome is gone, what happens to the girls? I feel sorry for them. Someone must help them. And, well, Pastor, I thought maybe you . . . And, truthfully, without Sheriff Schuette around I wasn't sure where else to turn."

Standing, Emil came around the desk and took a seat next to Liam. "Thank you for sharing. I will do everything possible to make sure that if there are girls being used that they get the help they need."

"Thank you, Pastor. And, I am sorry to interrupt your work."

"Liam, there is no need to apologize for anything, certainly not for sharing what you know. It's the only way to get to the truth."

Unable to immediately pull the typewriter back and finish the Christmas Eve sermon, Emil just sat in silence after Liam left the office. He was thankful that within less than twelve hours it would no longer be advent but

Christmas, at least on his calendar. Advent had proven to be incredibly long and he was ready to take his place at the manger and sing with the angels, *"Angels we have heard on high, Sweetly singing o'er the plains, And the mountain in reply, Echoing their joyous strains, Gloria in excelsis Deo; Gloria in excelsis Deo. "*

Eventually Emil was able to focus on writing again. Pulling the final page from the typewriter, Emil sat back in the chair and took a deep breath. Tomorrow was going to be long day and he needed every ounce of energy to maintain a high level of performance. Knowing that he should go home, he sat paralyzed. Several hours of Advent remained and home didn't feel like the right place. The right place was on the opposite end of town from the church.

The key slid into the hole effortlessly and with the simple roll of the wrist to the right the lock quietly moved free of the door jam, a twist of the doorknob and Emil was inside. There was no blast of warm air for the temperature was only a few degrees above freezing. Emil concluded that the last time he left he pushed the thermostat too far to the left, fifty degrees was too cold.

Stepping into the living room and leaving his coat on until it warmed up, he couldn't say, in the moment, why he returned to Al's house, other than something was luring him back. He stopped at the desk and opened the drawers he previously hadn't checked. There was nothing of significance stashed in drawers. It was all material that would eventually require his attention but not this afternoon.

Without a plan or an objective explaining why he was in the house, he worked his way upstairs and ended up in

Al's bedroom. He hadn't noticed earlier in the week when he entered the house that the bed was made and there were no dirty clothes anywhere in eye sight. He smiled to himself as he leaned against the wall and surveyed the room. Al was such a neat freak; everything was in its proper place. The same was true of the contents in the closet. A fifty-watt bulb lit the tiny space that held more than clothes. Two shelves above a wooden bar that held the hanging clothes contained boxes. Each box carefully placed on the shelf had been labeled with a black marker accept for a single box on the far right. The absence of words scrawled on the box created curiosity. Emil couldn't helpful himself; carefully he slid the box off the shelf. Cautiously removing the tape, which was meaningless since no one would question Emil's actions, the box was opened. Reaching inside he pulled out, what appeared to be a stack of letters and cards. Some bore a postmark and others must have been hand delivered since the envelope didn't carry a stamp. The items fell back into the box and Emil quickly returned the cardboard box to the stack as he couldn't force himself to read those private correspondences.

By the time the door closed behind him, Emil stood ridged less than halfway across the room. With his eyes closed his mind traced the words, *"My Dearest Allen."* It didn't register when he first read the envelope that someone used the name Allen, but outside the confinement of the closet, Emil realized that something wasn't right. But, it wasn't just the name Allen, that stopped him, it was the penmanship.

The box was placed on the bed and Emil lifted out several envelops. Shuffling quickly through the pile it was obvious each was written by the same person. Carefully opening one of the envelopes he pulled out the paper, unfolded it and started to read. He was shaking. He desperately hoped he was wrong.

My Dearest Love,

The minutes, the hours, the days since we were last alone together feels like years. My lips still tingle as I close my eyes and imagine you gently pressing yourself against me. I begin to sway as though we are dancing, and you are carrying me off to another place, another time. I don't know how much longer I can keep silent. Each time I see you my body swells with excitement and I want to sing. I want the whole world to know that I love you. Yes, I know the consequences, I know that others will be hurt but, are they not being hurt now by our lack of honesty?

The words I am about to share are the most difficult I have spoken to you since I first declared my love for you. I cannot continue like this, I just cannot, it is tearing me apart inside. We need to discuss our future, a future that is you and me, or we put an immediate end to this relationship. I love you so much, but I just cannot . . .

The letter ended abruptly. Folding the paper, he returned it neatly to the envelope, and as he did so, he wondered, was she interrupted or, was this intentional? And what about Al? Keeping these correspondences was so unlike him, but then he didn't plan on sharing them with anyone. Yet, Emil couldn't begin to count the times Al said it was the criminal's stupidity that lead to their demise. Was this stupidity or simply a person in love? Was there a difference? Emil smiled to himself for a second and then he remembered the lover. Why hadn't his lover retrieved the letters? Was she even aware that Al had been saving them? Perhaps she had tried, but he possessed the key, and therefore, her efforts would have been in vain.

Turning the box over, the letters and cards spilled across the bed. Emil was confident he knew the name of Al's lover, but he needed proof. His thought was that maybe an earlier letter or card would bear the woman's name. It was the type of evidence he would need to verify his suspicions.

The handwriting on the first dozen or more envelopes was significantly different from the letter he just read. There was no swoop on the letters ending each word. Emil concluded that these were older and possibly from an earlier lover. To read these letters and cards felt like he was invading their privacy.

Starting at what he hoped was one of the first correspondences, from the handwriting he recognized, he read this letter aloud.

I realize what we are doing is totally wrong, yet when I am with you it feels so right. I wasn't looking for this to happen it just sort of did.

Emil stopped and questioned the logic put forth. Therefore, since it just sort of happened, it made it okay, acceptable? Tossing the note aside without folding it, he selected a card. The cover, in big red letters, read, *To That Special Someone.* The handwritten message scrolled in blue ink inside the card matched the sentiment.

The other afternoon was wonderful. You swept me off my feet. I have yet to return to earth. Your lady in waiting . . .

The card was signed. It was the first time the woman's name appeared.

Katie.

Emil choked. He felt faint and his knees shook. The room started to turn. The card drifted back to the bed as it fell from Emil's fingers. He recognized her handwriting, but it was something entirely different to see her name. Like a punch in the gut. He was no longer sure it was a good idea to read the letters.

Tears distorted the words as he picked up another letter and tried to discern what his Katie was sharing with his best friend. He paused for a moment to clear his thoughts. As he wiped away the wetness from his face he wondered why he was doing this to himself. What was it about human nature that is a glutton for punishment?

The letter pressed between his fingers spoke of Al's uneasiness about what was unfolding.

It's been more than a month since you last made time for me. It has been a challenge to idly wait for you to work through the difficulty of this relationship. I refuse to call it an affair because that suggests we are merely taking advantage of one another for self-gratification. It is true that you make me feel like a woman again, that I am special but, I also want to give to you. I want to offer the same to you. You are struggling, because of Emil, you have said that repeatedly but, that doesn't change the fact of what we feel for each other.

Emil was unable to finish the letter. The weight and pressure of Katie's words drove him to the floor. He hit the floor with a thud, like a bale of hay tossed from the hay loft. Gaining some composure after a few minutes he turned and rested his back against the bed. The bed! Like a sludge hammer pounding a stake into packed soil, he found himself seeing the two of them on the bed. Based on the letter he still gripped in his right hand, he could only conclude that they had been intimate with one another. And if not by the time of the letter, certainly at some point moving forward.

His thoughts continued to swirl as though he was caught in the rapids of a river, the weight of the questions pulling him deeper and deeper under water. When did this first start? How did he not see it?

He grabbed another envelope from the box. The objective was simple; he hoped to establish a timeline of when this "affair" started. The envelope contained a recipe card and objective short message.

This may sound silly, but I think I have a solution to our dilemma of exchanging letters without getting caught. We use the couch. We will place letters under the cushions. When you stay overnight you can retrieve or deliver a letter.

That explained the transfer of letters but was there more to this? Emil shook his head immediately. Why was he being so foolish? Why attempt to minimalize the depth of this relationship? The truth he couldn't escape was the fact that he aided them in their correspondence. Many nights he insisted that Al stay and sleep on the couch. He went so far as to lay out the blankets and pillow.

Seated on the floor in Al's bedroom, next to the bed, he blamed himself for pushing them together, as though it was his fault. Feeling sorry for himself he became immobilized as he recalled the times he failed to treat Katie as a special person. As the self-pity swelled into anger, he did everything possible to avoid directing that emotion at either Katie or Al. What good would it do to be angry with Al? He was dead. Anger directed toward Katie was another issue entirely. But it wasn't anger he felt, it was . . . disappointment.

Initially Emil wondered how she could do this to him. But eventually he wondered how she could do this to herself? How could she dismiss her moral compass and permit herself to become caught up in a torrid affair? It was painful to admit, if she no longer loved him, so be it, she had every right to move on, but to engage in such a secretive relationship that would impact many more people than just the three of them was so uncharacteristic of Katie. What happened? When did it happen?

The letters and cards on the bed couldn't answer *what* happened, but he was sure there were clues in his wife's own handwriting to describe *when* it happened. As painful as it would be, Emil sat on the bed and proceeded to open every single envelope.

He discovered a side of his wife he never knew, or had refused to know. She wrote of dreams never shared with him. She described her struggle with being a pastor's wife. She hated living in a glass house. It pained her to always be on display and yet never seen as a woman who possessed gifts and talents apart from her husband. Their arguments made sense as he realized that she wasn't questioning his ministry as much as she was screaming to have a life of her own, an identity. Many letters spoke of being tired of being referred to as, *the pastor's wife.* She even wondered if people knew her first name.

As disheartening as it was, he acknowledged that Katie was similar to those young girls who found themselves searching for someone to affirm them. She wanted, she needed to be accepted and loved simply for who she was or had become.

Emil took a deep breath and scanned the room to calm

the waves of emotion. He stopped moving the moment he saw his reflection in the mirror attached to the dresser. He stared at himself for the longest time. Finally, he garnered the nerve to address the person in the mirror. He confessed to the face that didn't look like a pastor, but a man plagued with guilt. He was guilty of being everyone's pastor and not a pastor to his wife, or to himself, for that matter. He was guilty of being a pastor and not a husband.

Mindlessly reading another letter he screamed, "Oh, Katie!" The letter described the heroics of Al and the firemen as they rescued the livestock from the Vorweck barn. The fire, the result of a cigarette butt carelessly tossed aside, occurred a year and a half earlier. The relationship was at least eighteen months old. Six months after their arrival in Germantown, Katie and Al launched into a relationship.

Emil punished himself with sarcasm, "My god, after six months, I barely knew people's names let alone . . ." The one person Emil thought he knew, the one person he trusted, the one person he allowed himself to be vulnerable with, was the one person who would hurt him the most.

CHAPTER 20

Emil came home so late that he knew Katie wouldn't question why he slept in the den. The odds were she wouldn't question his absence; she could appreciate the weight of the sermons he had to prepare. But of course, it wasn't the writing of sermons that weighed him down, it was Katie herself.

Emil shuffled into the den and dropped his weary, fatigued body into the chair without removing his coat or flipping the switch to light the room. The cover of darkness was what he needed. He didn't need any reminders of who he was, instead, he needed to prepare himself, mentally and spiritually, for tomorrow. As much as he desired to sleep his thoughts traversed a broad spectrum. Among the images and words that occupied his mind was the sermon title for the Christmas Eve service, "In the Right Place." He needed to determine, before morning, if he was in the right place.

In lieu of everything he discovered earlier in the evening, he questioned the wisdom of having scheduled Al's funeral on Christmas Eve. Although, if he was honest, and he was trying very hard to be honest with himself, even without the letters and cards, did a Christmas Eve funeral make sense?

Vernon tried to persuade him to reconsider but he wouldn't hear it. Days earlier, it made perfect sense, but now…

He awoke to tiny beads of sweat rolling down the sides of his torso, as his overcoat was still three-quarters of the way buttoned. It was a tickling sensation that roused him from a dream. In his slumber, he and Al were chatting about the meaningless virtues of life when he felt Katie's fingers gently caressing his sides. But, neither Al nor Katie were present, he was merely overheated. Straining to read the wall clock in the darkness, he was eventually forced to cross the room, leaving his overcoat and one neatly pressed white shirt behind. The clock read two minutes after two. He hadn't slept for more than twenty minutes and yet, it felt as though it had been hours.

Returning to the chair, his body shook involuntarily with a slight chill as he was exposed to the night air. He draped the overcoat over his body and told himself he needed to fall back asleep. Unfortunately, images of Katie's handwriting flashed before him and it was only a matter of time before the overcoat was pushed downward as his body temp rose. What would he say to her when he saw her for the first time? As much as he might want, he couldn't avoid her indefinitely. Where did he begin? "Katie, I saw, I read . . ."

It was the stabbing pain in his shoulder blades that woke him. No matter how he attempted to position his body in the chair it was not comfortable. The muscles in his body were rebelling. The moment had arrived to get up no matter what time the clock on the far wall declared. Fortunately, it was 6:42 a.m.

Prior to drifting off to sleep Emil decided that to avoid Katie, for as long as possible, he would rise early and make himself breakfast before going upstairs to bathe and dress for the day. With any luck, Katie would be downstairs when he exited from the bathroom and he could dress in private and leave the house with a simple comment, "I'll see you at the church."

Emil knew Robert Burns' famous line from the poem, *To a Mouse,* "The best laid plans of mice and men often go awry." all too well. That was precisely what unfolded. Emil brewed a pot of coffee, made a small batch of oatmeal, and toasted two slices of bread, topped with peanut butter and grape jelly. With the kitchen at his back he crossed the dining room vigorously striding to the stairwell. As his left foot landed on the step and his right hand grabbed the railing, he directed his glaze upward and . . . there she stood.

Time stopped, the world ceased to spin, the earth no longer revolved about the sun. Who cared about traveling to the moon? Who cared if the Russians where in Cuba? Who cared…Emil cared and that was all that mattered.

Katie waited at the top of the stairs in flannel pajamas covered with a thin, raggedy green robe. As he proceeded upward, his right foot was followed by the left, then the right, then the left. He recalled the Christmas where a lone package behind the barren evergreen tree held the robe Katie wore.

The tree had been a gift from the owner of the corner hardware store. The shipment of Christmas trees arrived the Sunday before Thanksgiving. Emil heard the grain sized truck grind to a halt in front of the hardware store as the driver, impatient to make his delivery and move on to the next stop, laid on the horn with the hope of arousing someone from inside the building. At four o'clock in the morning with the temperature struggling to stay above freezing the wailing sound vibrated through the abandoned city streets as it bounced off the three and four-story brick buildings. Emil was in his final year of seminary and he and Katie were living on the third floor of one of those buildings. It was the newlywed's first Christmas.

Irritated by the inconsiderate behavior of the driver, Emil went to the window to determine for himself what would cause a person to act in such a manner. He pushed the curtain to one side to eliminate the distortion from the sheer fabric as the blaring stopped. What he witnessed, however, was a single individual laboring to pull five, six, even seven-foot evergreen trees from the back of the truck.

Unable to return to any form of peaceful slumber, Emil dressed in haste, exited the building, and crossed the street. Passing the door of the truck and finding the driver sitting smoking a cigarette, Emil stopped and asked why he wasn't helping unload the truck. After blowing smoke in his face, the driver informed Emil that his job was to bring the trees to the location, he wasn't paid to unload them. When Emil reached the back of the truck he found the owner of the hardware and climbed to the top of the stack of evergreens and began helping him unload.

As the driver pulled away, grinding the gears trying to find second, the owner of the hardware store and the make shift Christmas Tree lot, informed Emil that for his efforts he should stop by the tree lot the day before Christmas and he could pick any tree, at no charge, from what remained.

When Emil and Katie arrived at the tree lot on the twenty-fourth the selection had dwindled to less than a dozen. Emil whispered to Katie, who leaned in close to brace herself against the cold wind, "There are hardly any trees left, good for the owner, bad for us!"

Katie smiled and whispered back, "It doesn't matter which we choose, it will be the right tree."

The couple popped three kettles of popcorn and carefully strung the corn into garland to decorate the tree. Placed in the front window the street lights provided a glow through the huge gaps that existed between the branches. When Katie awoke the next morning, a single package rested against the trunk of the tree. Overwhelmed with emotion she busted into tears and confessed, "But I didn't get you anything."

Retrieving the gift from beneath the tree and presenting it to Katie, Emil informed her that it was actually a gift for both of them.

Lifting a green robe out of the box, Katie turned to Emil with her cheeks moist. She questioned how this was for both of them.

"Every time I see you wearing the robe I will always remember just how much I loved you that first Christmas…"

There she stood, at the top of the stairs wearing that green robe, faded and thread barren in spots, he was overwhelmed recalling the promise he made that he would always remember how much he loved her. Carefully stepping to the one side to pass by her without permitting their bodies to touch he said, "Maybe it's time you get a new robe."

With pencil in hand and Al's funeral sermon placed on the desk in the church office, Emil proceeded to rework the sermon. Less than a quarter of the way through the second page, Emil heard the arrival of the hearse. He grabbed his coat and headed for the front door knowing that Vernon would need his assistance bringing the casket inside and scaling the stairs into the sanctuary. Pulling Al's wooden casket out of the hearse took Emil's breath away. Until that moment, he had been able to view Al's funeral as any other member's funeral. But seeing the casket that he and Katie selected and realizing that he would never again share a beer, a good laugh, or a stressful moment, made him lose his balance. He fell to the ground and the casket dropped on top of him.

Vernon rushed to lift the weight off Emil and shouted, "Are you okay?"

Emil quickly righted himself and covered the truth with a plausible explanation. "Yes, yes, I am fine. I just slipped on some ice and I couldn't stop myself from going down. I guess Al is a little heavier than I thought."

Vernon helped Emil brush the snow from his backside and suggested that they take a moment before moving the casket inside.

Emil objected immediately, "No, seriously, I am fine. It's too cold out here to stand around. Let's get him inside and we can stop for a moment before we start up the stairs."

In the comforts of the narthex they set the casket down and Vernon's assistant returned to the hearse to retrieve the casket stand and start unloading the countless bouquets of flowers. Alone, Vernon looked at Emil and asked, "You okay? I don't just mean physically."

"Yes, I'm fine."

Resting his hands on the casket, Vernon leaned closer to Emil, "Don't give me that, he was your friend. A very good friend as I recall. What do you mean, you're fine? Look, in this business, I have to prepare the body of friends and if I am not honest with myself on how I am feeling, it hits me at the most unexpected times and it hits hard."

"So now, in addition to an undertaker, you're also a Psychiatrist?"

"No, I am only telling you what happens to me. And, since you are a pastor and not God, I assume things can also happen to you that you can't control."

"What are you getting at, Vernon?"

"Why are we doing this today?"

"What do you mean?"

"Stop playing dumb with me. I know there is more at work here than simply a funeral. There is no family involved so we could have scheduled this funeral for any time later this week. Why today? Today, Christmas Eve, of all days? You have another service less than five hours after this one, why?"

Emil walked backwards until he reached the steps and planted himself on the third step. "You promise this is just between you and me and it will never, never go any further."

"Come on, Emil, you know me."

"No, I need to hear you say it."

"Yes, of course, it doesn't go any further."

"Initially, it made sense. Christmas is about God coming to deliver us, humanity, from ourselves. What a funeral message, right? That was my motivation. Yet, there was something more driving this, I just couldn't name it. For a while, I thought it was the shock of Al's death. The desire to get his body in ground and move on, it would be less painful that way. But, I had this feeling that it was something more, something I couldn't name, I just knew it existed." Emil stopped as the assistant entered carrying the stand.

When the assistant was out of ear shot, Vernon inquired, "Was there, is there something more?"

"Oh yeah." The arrival of the assistant at the top of stairs silenced Emil yet again.

Vernon suggested that they carry the casket upstairs and then his assistant could bring all the flowers and flower stands into the narthex and he and Emil would assist in bringing them upstairs.

With Al's casket positioned at the base of the steps to the chancel, Vernon turned toward Emil and asked, "So, what more is there?"

Taking a seat in the front pew Emil didn't start at the beginning or the end of the story, instead he started with the words he needed to hear. "I guess a part of me knew. I knew that something was up, I just kept avoiding it."

After several minutes of silence, Vernon prompted Emil to continue. "What did you know?"

"That Al and Katie are . . ." Emil stopped himself, shook his head and continued, "were having an affair."

Vernon sat down next to his friend, "Oh . . . my . . . God . . . Emil, I am so sorry."

"Sorry, what are you sorry about? Unless of course, you knew. Did you know?" There was degree of anger in Emil's response.

"No, I didn't know. I am sorry that you have been put in such a predicament. I am sorry that you are experiencing such pain."

Nodding several times Emil spoke as his eyes stayed fixed on the cross. "Now, I am the one who must deliver the word, sorry. I am . . ."

Vernon stopped his friend before he could finish. "Stop.

There is no need. I wish we could finish this conversation but within less than an hour this place will be filled with people coming to pay their last respects. I have received calls all weekend from across the state inquiring about the time of the service and the location of the church. Despite it being Christmas Eve, the church is going to be packed, are you ready for that, Pastor?"

Emil stared at his hands, he turned them over several times. First he surveyed the palms and then the topside of his hands. When he finally looked up he said, "You know, Vern, I need it to be Christmas, we need it to be Christmas, the whole town needs it to be Christmas. I just hope that there is room in the manger for the Christ child."

CHAPTER 21

The sermon for Al's funeral remained front and center on Emil's desk. He struggled after his conversation with Vernon to determine if the corrections he had in mind were for himself or were words the community needed to hear? Reading the sermon for the tenth time the pencil in his right hand continued to find its way to the page. It was as though the lead was drawn to the paper. As several more sentences were darkened so as not to be delivered to the ears of the congregation, the front door slammed shut. The final review of Al's body wasn't scheduled to begin for another thirty minutes. Fearing that the person, or persons, who entered the narthex might be guests from a great distance, Emil decided he should investigate.

At the base of the stairwell stood four people Emil never imagined would attend the funeral, let alone enter the church. After a brief pause, Emil made is way down and met Detric Goldman in the middle of the staircase. He shook his hand and welcomed the family to First Lutheran Church. The initial conversation was stilted as neither man knew what should follow the welcome. It was Isaac who moved the conversation forward.

"We are here for Sheriff Schuette's funeral."

"Yes, yes, of course. The casket is upstairs. Thank you for coming."

It was Detric who spoke on behalf of the family. "Sheriff Schuette was a great man. He was one of the first people to welcome us to Germantown and many times he stopped violence against us. He did his job fairly and for that we are thankful. He treated us like human beings. If my boys..." Detric stopped long enough to push both boys, Isaac and Joshua, front and center, "did something wrong he held them to the law. That's the way it should be. The law is a gift from God. It helps us all live in peace. We now come to pay our respects to Sheriff Schuette."

Together the five of them climbed the stairs and walked the aisle to the casket. Emil stepped back as each member of the Goldman family stopped at the head and whispered what Emil assumed was a prayer. Joshua was the last and when he was finished he turned and spoke. "I know that no one is perfect, but besides my father, I know of no man who tried more to live his life following God's law."

Emil whispered, he couldn't speak aloud for fear his words would crack from the emotion that gripped his throat. "By God's law you mean, The Ten Commandments?"

"Yes," Joshua nodded.

Isaac stepped forward. "The words in our hearts and upon our lips today are Psalm 91. We . . ." Isaac stopped the moment he saw tears streaming down Emil's cheeks.

As he wiped the wetness from his face Emil apologized, "I'm sorry, but that is the Psalm I selected for today's service and it is the basis of my message."

Detric, with his arm around Emil's shoulders said,

"There is no need to apologize. God works in mysterious ways. It is not ours to question, but to believe."

Returning to his office, Emil picked up the pencil and snapped it in two and tossed it into the garbage. He was thankful that he had read the sermon ten times and knew it word for word as he had first written it.

Emil took his place beside the casket and looked out over the congregation. There wasn't room for another person to squeeze in anywhere. The front two pews on both sides of the aisle were filled with law enforcement personnel – and Katie. Vernon arrived and closed the casket in preparation for the start of the service while Emil read the opening verses of Psalm 91. *"He who dwells in the shelter of the Most High, abides under the shadow of the Almighty. He shall say to the Lord, 'You are my refuge and my stronghold, my God in whom I put my trust."*

The organist banged out the prelude to the opening hymn and Emil took a seat in the chancel behind the pulpit. With hymnal in hand, partially blocking his face, he eyed Katie. What was she was thinking? What was she feeling as she watched the cover close? He was surprised to note that neither her cheeks nor her eyes were moist. Perhaps she was all cried out.

When the time came in the service for the sermon, Emil stepped up into the pulpit and, following a brief prayer, delivered the sermon he wrote days earlier word for word. The theme was that Christmas isn't just the celebration of a baby born in a manger, but the promise of salvation, salvation delivered by and through the one born in the manger. The angels who announced the coming of Christ are the angels sent to watch over us. They are the same angels who watched over Al during his time on Earth and who continue to watch over Al in Heaven.

Less than a fifth of the people in church came to the cemetery service. The freezing temperatures had something to do with that. Fortunately, the early arrival of snow and the depth of the snow provided a thermal cover that kept the ground from freezing which enabled the grave digger to perform his duties. With Katie at his side, Emil spoke the time-honored words, "In sure, and certain hope to the resurrection of eternal life through Jesus Christ, we commend to Almighty God our brother, Allen Schuette, earth to earth, ashes to ashes and dust to dust we commit his body to his final resting place."

The moment Al's name was uttered, Emil felt Katie drop a few inches. He could only assume that she experienced what he had hours earlier, the weight of reality.

Silently, the cluster of mourners moved closer to one another and watched as the casket disappeared. As the top of the wooden structure reached ground level, Emil noticed a single yellow rose. The symmetry of the yellow petals against the dark grained wood fighting to stay alive in the frigid conditions made Emil's heart skip a beat. He could only assume the flower had been delivered by Katie, but he lacked any evidence to prove his suspicion. A fog of vapor, the result of exhaling, as multiple shovels of dirt were tossed into the hole, served as a reminder that every breath is a gift.

Busying himself greeting both visitors and members in the church basement following the committal, Emil didn't notice when Katie left the church. It was their practice not to sit together during such gatherings in order that people might not feel as though they were interrupting the couple when they approached the pastor. As the bowls of food were passed and coffee cups were drained, the somber mood was transformed. Pockets of laughter erupted as stories were shared, many starting with the words, "Remember when…" As the numbers slowly diminished it once again felt like Christmas Eve. People were ready to celebrate the holiday.

Switching off the basement lights before returning to his office, Emil thought about what Walter had said about the figurine and he hoped he was right, that it would be returned on Christmas day.

Walter was the first person to return to the church in preparation for the Christmas Eve Service. There were numerous small tasks to complete before the church bustled with anticipation of what the night might bring. Children would be giddy with excitement unable to control their bodies, parents would sit tall and proud cherishing the moment to once again see their entire family assembled in the pew, and grandparents would beam with delight thinking about days gone by and pondering what the future might hold for their grandchildren, great-grandchildren, and even great-great-grandchildren yet to be born. Christmas Eve was a magical night when the animals defied nature and spoke and people dreamed of a world filled with peace.

Wearing his coat, with his hat and gloves neatly tucked in the pockets, Walter stood in the doorway of the office and asked where the candles might have been placed following last year's Christmas Eve service. He had checked the sacristy without any luck and before heading to the basement to tear into the closet, he thought it best to ask the pastor if he knew where they were stored.

Before addressing the matter of the missing candles, Emil had to know if Walter noticed if the manger was still empty when he entered the church.

"Do you not trust that, had the figurine been returned, it would have been the first thing I said to you?"

"Yes, of course." Emil felt silly for asking the question. "Now, as for the candles, remember how we found the candles in the sacristy last year bent and melted together from the summer heat? We decide that they needed to be stored in a cool place. They're in the basement closet right below the small window."

"Pastor, I know you're disappointed, but you must be patient. If I am right about who took the figurine, I'm confident it will appear before the night is over." Walking out of the office, Walter added one last reminder. "Remember Pastor, patience."

By 6:15 p.m. the narthex swelled with noise. There was laughter, words of greeting exchanged between members who had not seen one another since last Christmas and members who, two hours earlier, had been here for the funeral. Children spoke of the wonders beneath the Christmas tree at home. And of course, people asked Pastor Fischer why there was no baby Jesus in the manger. The service didn't officially start for another forty-five minutes but members knew if they wanted an entire pew for their family they needed to arrive early. Before the service started there would also be twenty-five minutes of prelude music performed by the children of the congregation. The youngest musician was five and the oldest was a freshman in college.

The mimeograph machine in the office cranked out two dozen more bulletins when the ushers announced they were running short. Walter turned the crank as the pastor caught the pages and Rozella folded them. Emil learned the first year not to throw away the stencil.

Two minutes after seven, Emil stood before the congregation and offered an opening Christmas greeting and welcomed everyone to the Candle Light Christmas Eve Service. As he spoke, he quickly took note of who was present, and her absence was obvious. Directing his gaze to the balcony, thinking that perhaps she arrived late and went upstairs to find a seat, only added to his wonderment. She wasn't in the church, was she on her way? Was she overcome with grief? Was she… He needed to focus, there would be time later to address her absence. At that moment it was not about her it was about those who *were* present.

Three rows back from the front, on the right side in the middle of the pew, sat Stanley and Greta Dempewolf clinging to one another for the first time in who knows how long. Across the aisle and one pew further back were the Arendt's, minus, of course, their son, David. Next to them in the same pew were the Hillman's. Oh, Vanessa, it would only be a matter of time before the entire town learned of her condition. Karl Mueller and his family filled an entire pew on the right side and directly behind Karl sat Liam Mueller. Rozella Pagel found a comfortable seat next to her sister and brother-in-law, Marc Gerke. Lina Lietzau and her two children sat in the very last pew under the balcony in hopes of concealing their presence. Directly in front of them was the Grack clan. Vernon Kockelmeier sat in the front pew, not by choice but because it was the only place left when he arrived one minute after seven. Vernon shared the pew with Sarah Stark who, with the assistance of Walter, brought Veda to church to celebrate what no doubt would be her last Christmas Eve Service. And of course, Walter, he stood in the back of the church making sure everything went smoothly. He never told anyone, but he liked to think of himself as the director of the orchestra. The Christmas message had been written for these people, for those who had gathered to celebrate Christmas and not for those missing.

For the second time within less than five hours, Emil climbed into the pulpit to share God's word. Following a brief prayer, he began.

"Upon the shepherds' arrival in Bethlehem they proceeded to share with Mary all they had heard and seen, the text says at that point, 'Mary pondered all these things in her heart.'"

"What do you suppose Mary pondered? Might it be that as she looked about she questioned if this was the right place to deliver the Savior of the world?

What does a mother, any mother, ponder at the birth of her child?

I confess to you this night that I have spent the season of Advent pondering. It started with the consternation of when to place the figurine in the nativity. It...

We, as a country, this past year have pondered the future of civilization. With the arrival of the Soviet Union . . .

If we are honest, we must admit that we don't know all what Mary pondered in her heart, but we do know she pondered the words, 'for unto you is born this day, in the city of David, a Savior.'

And so, it is that we, you and I, ponder the angelic proclamation, for unto you is born this day in a place that we ponder, a Savior. For unto you is born this day in your heart a Savior. Mary pondered all these things in her heart. The heart is God's new manger where the Christ child, where Jesus, is born and lives. It is the right place.

The angelic proclamation this night is that, for unto you is born this day in your heart a Savior! A Savior to deliver you from all that threatens to destroy you, from all that threatens to weigh you down, from all that threatens to burden your heart with senseless pondering, from all that threatens to separate you from the love of God.

Hear it again, for unto you to is born this day in your heart a Savior! It is the right place for the Savior of the world to reside.

Dropping into the chair behind the pulpit while the congregation sang, "Away in a Manger," Emil took a deep breath and contemplated what Katie was pondering in her heart? He realized he couldn't save her, nor could she save herself, that job alone belonged to Christ. Yet, he also realized that he couldn't permit her to separate herself from the only source that could make her whole again. The words to the final verse of the hymn, "Be near me, Lord Jesus; I ask you to stay . . ." brought Emil back into the church and focused his heart and mind for the remainder of the service.

The instructions for the lighting of the candles were direct, "Tip the unlit candle into the flame of the lit candle. Do not tip a lit candle as it will drop hot wax. The ushers will make their way down the center aisle and Walter will bring a lit candle to the balcony. Once all candles are lit we will continue the service by reading, in unison, the Christmas Prayer."

Emil stood patiently waiting for every candle to be lit and for the lights to be dimmed. With a nod from Walter at the back of church Emil invited the people to join in reading the prayer.

"Emmanuel, God with us, we bring to the manger hopes and dreams of all the years. We bring to the manger our own hopes and dreams. We pray that the Jesus manger would refocus our gaze, and align our hopes and dreams with the hope and dream you have, God for us and this world – a dream of peace, togetherness, kindness, and love. We pray for every day manger miracles that come from the Lord of Life, Jesus Christ. Amen."

Before Emil could instruct the congregation that the first verse of "Silent Night" would be sung in German, the organ softly played the introduction. On cue the congregation sang.

"Stille Nacht! Heil'ge Nacht!
Alles schlaft, einsam wacht
Nur das traute hoch heilige Paar.
Holder Knab' im lockigen Haar,
Schlafe..."

The first verse had yet to conclude when Walter rushed down the center aisle calling out, "Pastor Fischer, the baby! Pastor Fischer, the baby!" The people grew silent and the organist lifted her fingers from the keys at the most inopportune moment. Emil stepped down from the chancel and met Walter who was out of breath.

Patting Walter's back Emil asked him to repeat himself.

"The baby, the Christ child, the figurine is in the manger. Come, come see."

A gasp filled the church followed by whispers of, "What did he say?"

Cautiously Emil asked, "Is it our figurine?"

"Yes, come see." Walter was halfway down the aisle waving for Emil and the people to follow.

Motivated by excitement Emil's stride was twice that of a normal walk giving the illusion that his alb had angelic qualities as it flowed behind him. Into the night air the congregation gathered. Many of the people stood knee deep in snow but not a single soul complained. Silence gripped each person as they looked at the nativity scene and considered how their heart was the new manger.

No one could say for sure who started it, but the entire group began to sing once again, Stille Nacht. The first verse was in German followed by the remaining verses in English. The river valley, Germantown, was filled with the joyous sound of Christmas. With a single strike of a wooden match candles were lit and held high to light the night and announce the arrival of the baby Jesus. For a brief interlude the cozy village tucked in the bluffs along the Minnesota River was the ideal place to celebrate Christmas.

CHAPTER 22

Emil pulled up to his house still hearing Marcia Miller regaling the worshippers with, "O Holy Night." Although the temperature was well below freezing the people lingered next to the Nativity scene. No one, not the young or the old, wanted to return indoors. Everyone simply pressed closer together to share the warmth from one body to another. There was something captivating being a part of the Nativity. For a fleeting second Emil entertained the idea of suggesting that next year the church should create a live nativity, but he quickly dismissed that thought acknowledging that the council needed time to recover from the events surrounding this year's nativity scene. In spite of all the hassles and stress created with a new baby Jesus figurine, Emil knew that the money spent for the figurine was money well spent.

People speculated, as they began to disperse, that Walter, or the Pastor himself, was responsible for the disappearance of the figurine. It made sense considering how at the right moment the baby was returned. It made sense considering that every investigation turned up nothing. It made sense except for the fact that, neither Walter nor Emil had actually taken the figurine.

Emil set the parking brake and shoved open the metal car door. The hinges groaned against the wintery conditions and he looked up and realized that the only source of light in the house came from the Christmas tree. The lights cast a twinkling glow through the partially frosted picture window. Following the crooked path, one foot carefully placed in front of the other, Emil stopped to admire the twinkling stars. The heavenly sky was littered with countless glimmering lights. The night air driven by a slight breeze propelled the crisp particles of moisture through the cracks of his clothes until they struck his body. It was strangely refreshing to bask under the stars of Heaven and to feel such warmth inside his body while the outside was popping with goosebumps. It reminded him of sitting with David and dreaming, traveling and never leaving the hospital room. It reminded him of being a kid playing outdoors, building a snow fort, or ice skating in the ditch, freezing his ears and hands to the point he no longer felt them and the joy of sharing that moment with his grandpa. It reminded him of the first time he saw Katie walking across the room. His insides bubbled like boiling water and his outside was frozen stiff like a rodent that didn't make it back to cover. Even at that moment, the thought of Katie created that contradiction in his body.

Rubbing his hands along the arms of his coat created friction and heat while the notion of contradiction stuck with him. Tomorrow the house would overflow with people. His family and Katie's family would arrive early in the morning. The entire house, from the basement to the attic, would be lit with every possible lightbulb aglow. The entire house would be filled with people playing, laughing, an occasional child screaming or crying, and everyone, everyone enjoying the concept of family. What awaited him on the other side of the front door was darkness and silence, loneliness and abandonment, Katie and no one else.

One foot carefully placed in front of the other, Emil moved toward the front door. Surprised to discover the door locked he removed his glove to dig through his pants pocket to locate the skeleton key. With speed he stepped inside and rushed to close the door as the outside attempted to pull as much heat as possible from the house. The warmth felt good against his face and the smell of fresh pine was pleasing to his nose. After draping his coat over the back of the chair and setting his rubbers between the chair's legs, Emil cautiously stepped into the living room.

The couch, the place Al had spent many nights, was turned towards the Christmas tree. In the center of the couch Katie sat with her legs tucked under her nursing a tall glass of red wine. She never moved, she didn't utter a word as her husband approached the back of the couch. Lightly, as though touching an unexpected wild creature for the first time, Emil placed his hands on her shoulders and at the same time kissed the back of her head.

"Merry Christmas." He whispered the words so as not to destroy the space she had created for herself. He felt as though he was a guest and it was up to her to invite him in.

"Is it?" The words were colder than the air that numbed his body.

He wasn't about to debate if it was Christmas, it was. As for Merry, perhaps it wasn't cheerful or joyous, but he wasn't about to debate that either. Instead, he focused on that which was factual. "The baby Jesus was returned."

"Yes?"

"You?"

"Yes." Her body didn't move an inch.

"Why?"

She pulled away from his hands and scooted to the end of the couch so she could look directly at him. "Why, what? Why did I steal it? Or, why did I return it?"

Still kneeling at the backside of the couch Emil spoke calmly. "If you are willing, I would like to hear an answer to both."

"Oh my god, don't you ever get mad, don't you ever lose control? Don't you ever want to shout and scream? 'If you are willing?' What kind of crap is that?"

With a shrug of his shoulders he answered, "Katie, what good would it do if I shouted or screamed? As for being mad? I'm not mad, I'm hurt."

"HURT?" She shouted at him. "You don't know the meaning of hurt. At least if you shouted and got mad I'd know I was married to a man and not married to someone trying to be God. I stole the figurine because I am tired. I am sick and tired of being married to the church. I hate being a pastor's wife. I hate living in a glass house. I hate that people call me, 'the pastor's wife.' I hate…" she stopped herself for a moment. She swallowed hard and continued, "I hate you for letting this happen and I hate myself even more for feeling this way. I hate myself because…" Again, she stopped herself but this time she did not continue.

From past experiences Emil understood that Katie's words were not seeking a response but a spewing forth of emotion. To respond would have made matters worse. She didn't need a rebuttal but compassion, understanding, mercy. She needed someone to be merciful and he offered just such a gift in the form of silence.

His knees hurt from kneeling on the wooden floor, so he stood and as he did he noticed another glass, an empty glass, was on the coffee table next to the bottle of wine. He squeezed his body between the coffee table and the couch and took a seat on the opposite end of the couch from Katie. He poured himself some wine and savored the taste as it warmed his throat.

In silence, they stared at the lights on the tree for the better part of thirty minutes. Without uttering a word or looking up, Katie slid her body, wrapped in the raggedy green robe, across the couch until she was next to her husband. She removed the glass of wine from his hand and took his arms and wrapped them about her body. As she leaned against him she spoke of the figurine. "I hid the figurine in the attic in a box marked wedding items. I was confident if anyone assumed you took the baby Jesus they would never open that box."

A box marked wedding items; he couldn't help but ponder the irony, for them as a couple, and the image of Christ as the bridegroom and the people as his bride. He also noted how she never assumed that anyone might consider she was the thief, therefore, he had to ask, "And Al, did Al ever question you about the figurine?"

"Al?" There was tension and nervousness in her voice as she spoke his name. He felt her body stiffen against him. "Why are you mentioning Al?"

Her ear was close to his mouth, so he spoke softly. "After the first week of the figurine's disappearance, Al avoided any discussion about it. I had a feeling he knew precisely where it was, but he refused to say anything. Did he know you had it?"

She emptied her glass before answering and didn't make eye contact with him. "He never questioned me about the figurine. I have no idea if he knew I had it, but he was a good . . ." Katie paused.

Before Katie could complete the sentence, Emil finished it for her. "A good detective."

"Yes, a good detective." Her body relaxed as she spoke, and she again pressed against him.

"He will be missed by everyone."

Katie never responded, and Emil didn't need her to.

Long before Katie grabbed his hand and led him upstairs, Emil knew he was in the right place.

EPILOGUE

In every community, every church, every family there are secrets. Some of those secrets have the power to kill, some have the power to alter the future, some have the power to expose and even convict the guilty, and some, unfortunately, some secrets remain hidden for generations.

"Thanks be to God that God didn't keep the arrival of his son a secret."

Those were the words Pastor Fischer shared with the church council when they assembled in the library for the January meeting. He suggested that next Christmas the congregation should create a living Nativity. The gasp heard about the wood table told Emil that indeed, he was *In the Right Place!*

Also written by Douglas Knick:
The Kingdom of Collectible Treasures
The Mist Of Salvation
Horses in Heaven

ACKNOWLEDGEMENTS

In the Right Place would never exist without the following people. Thank you to Reverend Robert Dahl for reminding me of the work of Greg Boyle during a sermon on the Beatitude which eventually came to serve as the title of this book. It is with tremendous gratitude that I say "thank you" to Daniel F. Allen for granting permission to use his painting for the book cover. Daniel's studio is located in Northfield, MN, and he frequently displays his work at St. Olaf and Carlton Colleges, also located in Northfield, MN. It is always refreshing to work with the professionals at Ten16 Press. Shannon Ishizaki, the owner of the company, is always available at the drop of a hat. Kaye Nemec, my editor, patiently offers suggestions and corrections that add clarity to the book and challenges me to remember the reader. Finally, there are no words that can capture the support and love my wife, Tammie, offers as I labor through the journey of writing another book.

www.ingramcontent.com/pod-product-compliance
Lightning Source LLC
Chambersburg PA
CBHW031956240626
47153CB00003B/1006